WARNING!

The contents of this book are not politically correct.

Proceed at your own risk.

If you get your itty bitty feelings hurt, it is no business of the author. Grow up.

You've been warned.

Best regards,

Shelf Barker

I0618573

CRASH COURSE

A Shelf Barker Mystery

By Nicky McBride

Muffin Dog Press

For Andy Davies (ADI), without whose assistance neither this book nor the presence of a Reformed Yank on the roads of the United Kingdom would have been even remotely possible.

Disclaimer

Bill Lind, "The Origins of Political Correctness," *Accuracy in Academia* website, Feb. 5, 2000:

> Political Correctness is cultural Marxism. It is Marxism translated from economic into cultural terms. It is an effort that goes back not to the 1960s and the hippies and the peace movement, but back to World War I. If we compare the basic tenets of Political Correctness with classical Marxism the parallels are very obvious.

Both, Lind noted, are totalitarian ideologies, and therefore not in accord with the aims of free societies.

Nonetheless, any non-politically correct statements which may be expressed in this book are not the opinions of either the author or the publisher, but are part of the character(s) invented to carry the story to its conclusion.

Foreword

Consider the man on horseback, and I have been a man on horseback for most of my life. Well, mostly he is a good man, but there is a change in him as soon as he mounts. Every man on horseback is an arrogant man, however gentle he may be on foot. The man in the automobile is one thousand times as dangerous. I tell you, it will engender absolute selfishness in mankind if the driving of automobiles becomes common. It will breed violence on a scale never seen before. It will mark the end of the family as we know it, the three or four generations living happily in one home. It will destroy the sense of neighbourhood and the true sense of Nation. It will create giantized cankers of cities, false opulence of suburbs, ruinized countryside, and unhealthy conglomerations of specialized farming and manufacturing. It will make every man a tyrant. —R.A. Lafferty, "Interurban Queen," 1970, a short story set in the late 1800s

CRASH COURSE
Table of Contents

ONE

Drive My Car

Of all the jobs on earth, the best one is probably "born rich and feckless."

The second best is driving instructor. I can say this with a certainty born of three things.

First, I was not born rich, just feckless.

Second, I am lazy as hell, and I get to sit on my sainted bum all day long, waking up just long enough to express concern and correction although my body often wants to express an adrenaline rush worthy of an Al Qaeda bomber sighting. Not always. But consider: Could it be that not all humans are meant to drive? Could some not really be walkers, or even crawlers, who have drunk the Kool-Aid and think that it is their god-given right to drive, regardless of the resulting mayhem for society? If any national government had wanted to put driving students on the international terrorism list, it's almost certain other nations would have stepped up to help the Yanks crush them, at least if driving instructors had anything to say about it.

Moreover, because more people turn 18 globally every day, the war on road terror would be at least as endless as Afghanistan and Iraq. I realize this is greedy; I already have an endless supply of driver wannabes. But who knows? Maybe my offspring will want to become driving instructors, and if they did, I wouldn't want them to fall on hard times. The fact that I have no offspring notwithstanding.

Third, and most importantly, I have been through a number of other careers, many of them entertaining to my mind—university professor, dog walker, sandwichboardman, yoga teacher—and others uplifting to my spirit. On that last, meditation consultant comes immediately to mind. I admit that I could sit on my bum most of the day when I did that so I could be as feckless as I pleased while observers thought I was doing a hard day's work, but it was boring. No adrenaline to speak of. What I got out of it was an ex-wife who I think came up out of a woven basket when someone played a flute someplace down the hall in the ashram-like natural health and healing centre where I did my consulting. I had begun calling her The Cobra, behind her back, long before we split up. For a while, I couldn't even watch nature shows on the telly if they dealt with snakes, or even amphibians. I'm much better about it now, though. I can watch anything concerning snakes or snake-like creatures, although I draw the line at eating eels, and, fortunately, I don't know very many people who would eat—never mind make—traditional British jellied eels and serve the foul and gelatinous mess to anyone.

###

One of the most frightening things about your true nerd, for many people, is not that he's socially inept—because everybody's been there—but rather his complete lack of embarrassment about it.— *Neal Stephenson*

###

After a few months of consulting on meditation, I had to give up sleeping. Sleeping was very little different from what I did all day, so why do it? No, at night I prowled the neighbourhood. Do you have any idea how many people sneak their trash into neighbour's wheelie bins in the average British city neighbourhood? Why? I wondered. In my previous incarnation as a professor, I might have studied the issue. As it was, I simply collected the information against the possibility that it would come in handy at some future date. If one of the urban "fly tippers" annoyed me, for instance, I could threaten to tell their dirty secret to the bin's owner unless they ceased. Naturally, this also upset The Cobra. She thought I should be peaceful 24/7 but that just isn't in my nature. She also regarded my intelligence-collecting activities as tantamount to organized crime. She didn't care much for organized crime, not then, and even less more recently for reasons that will become clear if you stick with it long enough to find out who I really am. I don't mean that in the sense of how important I am, but in the sense of how truly pathetic I am. At the time, I pointed out that I was doing it alone, and one of her other complaints about me is that I am disorganized. Ergo....

I'm so disorganized, I have a hard time remembering my own name, or so The Cobra used to tell me in some of her more judgmental moods. My name is, in fact, Graham Barker. No middle name. My parents were Trostkyites and thought a middle name was too bourgeois. So, unlike other kids, I didn't have the choice of answering to Higginbotham or Smythe, or even Cedric, after a preferred second name. But I do answer to Shelf, a nickname that got hung on me, like the prices on a mega-store display, during one of my very early jobs stocking groceries from midnight to eight a.m.

People have asked me why I gave up being a university professor, especially considering the panoply of other jobs, some of them lousy, that kept the wolf from my door. It's easy. I was bored. While dogs come in all shapes and sizes, no two alike, and yoga students come in every version of fat and middle-aged there is, plus a few toothsome young things, university students are cookie cutter. Students come only in a range of a few types, and all of the students fit a type one way or another. No exceptions, whether the university is Essex University of Advanced Breakfast Bap Studies or Cambridge.

There is the artsy type, affecting black clothing, minimal adornment whether male or female, sketchy hygiene, dog-eared copies of both Jean Paul Sartre's complete opus and a working copy of *Spamalot* that they are mining for japes to use in their comparative history class. In this, they study the question of whether Henry the VIII really had much on Jack Kennedy in terms of lust and power. Usually, they've written a paper on Jack (John Fitzgerald) Kennedy suggesting that Jackie—Jacqueline Bouvier Kennedy Onasis—was his Catherine of Aragon but he didn't divorce her simply because he hadn't got round to it before he was murdered. Jumpin' Jack Flash (love that song…Kennedy is OK, too) was a lot less agile, as it turns out, than well-hung—albeit syphillitic—Hank; Jumpin' Jack had injuries suffered in WWII that made him a virtual cripple, not at all fast on his feet, so that ministrations by harlots visiting his castle had to suffice….Jackie put up with it. But then, her taste in men was questionable, considering her second marriage to a Greek shipping magnate who looked like a miniaturized Jabba the Hutt, and whose money had previously attracted opera divas. Gold? Jackie could understand gold. Men? Not so much.

Another university type is the chirpy female, enrolled not for a degree one would recognize by its acronym (PhD, for example) but for her Mrs. She tends to look a lot like Rene Zellweger in *Bridget Jones's Diary*.

There is the posh guy, the one whose public school education to date cannot be denied, if not in his plummy tones alone, then in his studiously casual couplings of clothes fit for sailing with those intended for society weddings. That is, he might wear a well-cut grey suit, but on his feet will be a pair of banged up boat shoes. Or he'll toss a pricey wool blazer on over his baby lime knitted shirt and khakis. The posh guy's colours tend to be just off basic, but not so trendy as mustard and puce. Shoes are always slip-ons of a very flimsy cut, suggesting that he walks only on thick-pile carpets or priceless old mahogany floors that won't bear any scratching, or boat shoes. Never trainers, unless, of course, he is actually training. A sweat suit and Velcro-closure trainers? On what planet, one might ask, would such a peacock among men wear such dross?

I admit, I often notice shoes. British men's shoes are world-famous, but only the Savile Row sort that go with bespoke business suits, or boat shoes. Casual men's shoes and virtually all women's shoes manufactured in the UK are rubbish. I know first-hand about the men's casual shoes. The women's shoes? Well, all my wives complained, and then when I met my current wife, the American, I saw what they meant. She goes back to the States just to buy shoes. Not even expensive shoes, just shoes. I don't know why the UK can't make a pair of well-fitting, comfortable, stylish women's shoes, but it can't. In a pinch, my wife will order from James English, which carries American brands like Sofspots and Naturalizer. Those shoes are OK, comfy and well-fitting. But they lack a little in the style department. You won't find the virtual leather-covered stilts, for example, that were passing for women's fashion shoes in the first decade or so of the current century. Nothing with fur around the ankles and tent laces up the front. Nothing, in short, on the extremes of fashion. But stylish? Yes, of course.

Did I mention my wife is stylish? Lord, yes. She doesn't go round as mutton dressed as lamb. And I doubt you'll ever get her into a hair salon that does blue rinses, no matter how long she lives. And John Lewis' range of clothing is just about *au courant* enough for her. She has about a dozen university degrees (OK, two), but you'd take one look at her shoes, now or when she was student-age I suspect, and you'd never guess she was a serious student. Speaking of which...

There is the serious student these days, the one—male or female—who has ingested whole sections of the library each evening in order to find the one quote on your subject you will probably not have ever heard of because you didn't swallow a library for your own degrees, but rather got them in the usual way, by sucking up to your own professors.

There is the over-reaching son/daughter of a steam-fitter who is both proud of and embarrassed by her family's humble status. This, in fact, makes this the most interesting of the types, providing they can keep their earnestness and their proclivity to issue bad-ass remarks in balance.

There is the athlete, although who ever defined cricket as a sport (sport being generally defined as a pursuit requiring movement) is about as likely to have actually ever seen sport as the person who has defined American football as sport. Cricket is a good opportunity to cat nap outdoors in a gentle breeze, and that includes players as well as spectators. Indeed, at some matches I've been obligated to attend (because I was the coach of the small college team, everyone else having been on holiday when the provost had to announce the faculty appointments for such things), it looked as if half the spectators were in deep comas. But they did arise and walk at the end of the game...unless someone had invented a 'quickening' machine over the duration.

American football should just be televised worldwide when someone wants to start a war. You have these veritable tanks in every possible hue of human skin, rolling toward each other over an open space. Each side carries its own flag, so to speak, on its gaudy helmets. Call one side Palestine, if you will, and the other Israel. Whoever wins gets to decide where the boundaries will be until the next game, next season, when it begins again.

I see a lot of hope for this. Look at all the money that could be saved on ordnance. Look at all the lives that could be saved. And the masses could be entertained at the same time. Plus, there's money in it for organized crime. Forget sanctioned betting shops, like BetFred in the UK and OTB in the States (which is only horses, anyway, I think). Let the Mafia do it. Then there would be substantial collateral damage, enough for Faux News to report so that the masses could have their daily dose of disaster for a while. Plus, no one would have to care about it, because who can, actually, care about people named Rafaello "The Candy Man" Rivello or Peter "Canned Heat" Bignarelli? Those aren't people; they're cartoons. You get the picture: the Road Runner zooming around a mountain and running Blam! into a tanker full of molasses and getting flattened on the tarmac.

So it's interesting, you know. The Mafia. The more Mafia there is around, the more you get interesting stories in the newspaper, because those guys—Riviello and Bignarelli—never die in bed. They are always found because the frost heaved the ground and suddenly a tell-tale diamond ring popped out of the dirt under the driveway of the new grammar school. Or a guy fishing for his dinner brought up an old shoe, with the foot still inside. Stuff like that.

We have very little Mafia in the UK, so I had to read US and Canadian newspapers to get a dose of mob speak every now and again. For instance, in November last year, the body of an alleged Mafia boss was fished out of a river north of Montreal. Naturally, he had a nickname, and naturally he also had a legitimate business—steel, as I recall. He was one of the Bonannos, but obviously not the top Bonanno (sorry) or he wouldn't have been croaked. The fact is, this guy was a true "global citizen." He had been born in Montreal, and raised in Sicily. He moved to the U.S. but never obtained U.S. citizenship. That was so interesting. Maybe he had one of the famous green cards? He couldn't have gotten it by working for a corporation, which is how many Brits do it. If they want to.

Or he could have married a U.S. citizen. Considering he rose early and far in the Sicilian organization, I guess he could have been attractive to a young woman looking for a successful businessman to father her children. In fact, he had three kids, but was deported to Canada in 2009 anyway after being convicted for refusing to testify before a grand jury on illegal gambling. Didn't seem to do him any good, being up there with all those unnaturally polite Canadians. Unless, of course, they said, "Excuse me, we are going to eliminate you now, eh?" before pumping and dumping him. He was legal in Canada, if not particularly desirable. So maybe some polite wise guys did the northern nation a favour.

It's not inconceivable that I'll get croaked in my job, either. But it won't be over territory, unless you consider England's roadways to be territory. And it probably won't be particularly polite, either. Sometimes I get visions of how it could go down.

For example, maybe someday I'll simply lose it if I get another student like Raymond. Raymond suffered from Asperger's syndrome and dyspraxia. Asperger's? Difficulties in social interaction, although that's the simplistic explanation. Put it this way; the behaviour of sufferers makes the term wallflower seem ebullient by comparison. Dyspraxia—simplistically—is the inability to plan and carry out various physical functions.

So, OK. Asperger's wouldn't necessarily be an impediment to driving, just to learning to drive. You can drive alone and not worry about making small talk, but you can't learn that way. You'll have to talk with the instructor, whether it's mum or dad or a hireling like me. Dyspraxia…well, it is estimated that as much as ten percent of the population suffers from it, so it's actually a wonder there are not a lot more prangs than there are.

Raymond had both syndromes bad. Early on, I realized he would need a lot more than 20 course hours; shortly I realized I couldn't explain the numerous things he did wrong directly, as he would all but curl up into a ball or alternatively sit with chin in hands for what seemed like hours thinking of the best answer to questions I asked. Eventually, I mixed up my approach between nagging and questioning and did it gently, and he began to trust me. He would even sometimes smile at my sense of humour, proof that at least one person thought it was amusing for me to say, "You are driving me round the bend, Raymond," when I wanted him to negotiate a curve.

###

"If a seed of a lettuce will not grow, we do not blame the lettuce. Instead, the fault lies with us for not having nourished the seed properly."—Buddhist proverb

###

My wife thinks I'm a natural teacher because of the ways I find to teach even tough cases to drive. I think it's self-preservation. I couldn't imagine sitting for hours with an incommunicative berk of any sort. To save my own sanity, I had to get them to talk. This was not, of course, at all difficult when I was at the university; students tended to talk right through the lecture, which gave one to wonder if they had been raised by wolves. But no, just by modern parents who didn't want to stifle their precious offsprings' creativity by teaching them to be attentive and polite.

Frankly, teaching took a lot out of me, whether at the babbling university, the spiritually silent bogus ashram or the modest learner car in which I now spent most of my days. In the L-car scenario, never doubt that the presence of Bulpitt made it worse. Indeed, his decisions regarding Raymond are a case in point.

Who is Bulpitt? The aptly named director of the vaunted institution at which I ply my current trade, John Wayne Bulpitt.

When Raymond was finally ready for his test, I told Bulpitt I HAD to be the instructor with Raymond as he would fail otherwise. Bulpitt, being Bulpitt, made sure I was unavailable. Needless to say, Raymond failed. If it had taken him 20 weeks to get used to me, how was this guy who would be called a social misfit in any other age going to trust someone he had known for ten minutes before the test?

Mainly, I don't like sitting in the car with the student during a test, but for the Raymonds, I make exceptions.

Next time Raymond had a test booked, I bulldozed Bulpitt and went with Raymond. He came close to failing a couple of times during that fraught 40 minutes of intense scrutiny by one of Her Majesty's roadworthiness examiners, but squeaked through. Since then he has completed an advanced course, too. Maybe it is helping him with the social thing. I don't know. It isn't Raymond that I want to kill; it's Bulpitt.

If I tried to kill Raymond, he'd just clam up and be so pitiful, I'd have to give it up. If I tried to kill Bulpitt, he'd probably turn all his cunning against me, not to mention the skills he might recall from his time in Great Britain's SAS. SAS stands for Special Air Services, and they make even Royal Marine Commandos look like ordinary grunts by comparison. They are indeed the elite in the killing fields to which they are sent. Bulpitt claimed to be an ex-SAS. I wouldn't know. Their faces are apparently never shown in photos, and I doubted very much that Bulpitt would pull out his warrant card, or whatever form of ID they use, to show me. He just mentioned it often enough to be slightly menacing. So, anyway, if I tried to kill him, the odds would be so far against me that even on his worst day, and my best….and even if I had a weapon and he didn't…well, I'd like a simple service, not too many flowers, and no maudlin hymns.

But I digress. This has nothing…well, little…to do with letting you know what sort of milieu I come from. (I love the word milieu, and hardly ever get to use it. It would ruin my tough-guy image. What tough guy image? Didn't I just tell you I was a feckless wastrel former academic, so how tough could I be?)

So, then, back to academia….

Virtually every student is a variation on one of these themes: Goth, artsy, chirpy, serious, posh, athletic. Some are more intelligent than others, but IQ really has no bearing on the interest they hold for a professor. Virtually all of them save their deepest angst for the university health service shrink or their current partner or possibly a psychiatrist in private practice or a woo-woo practitioner from a religion in rebirth (druidry, Methodist fundamentalism). Bored professors see little more than the sub-standard papers the students write, and hear little more than the latest lame excuse as to why the student couldn't even manage to buy a half-decent paper from an "academic research" company and get it in on time. Mainly, I suspect, it's because they had to cajole mum or dad out of the money to buy the work, and it took some time. Perhaps it had to wait for a trip home with the laundry.

Dog-walking was slightly more interesting. While all Jack Russells are pretty much alike (nuts, yappy, amusing) and all Labradors are pretty much alike (sane, quiet, boring), there are enough breeds of dog—and enough owners with agendas they impart to said dogs—to keep it amusing.

For example, I used to walk an Alsatian cross named Biff. I will grant you, it sounds made up. But it's not. Biff was the beloved pet of a little old lady who named him that because she could make him bark when she was on the phone or when there was a knock at the door and yell, "Down, Biff. I realize you haven't been fed yet today...." And so on, trying to make would-be miscreants back off *a priori*.

As it happens, I own Biff now. The old lady died, and when she did, she left Biff to me in her will. I'm a cat person at heart, so I wasn't keen on having an Alsatian of any sort. Alsatians eat cats, don't they? Anyway, being the soft-hearted divvy I am, I had no choice but, when the RSPCA called me, to take Biff home with me. This was actually two Biffs back. So sue me. I found I liked having a dog, and Biff was a good name for a dog owned by a yoga instructor. At least, it seemed to be when I was walking home through some rough neighbourhoods in my yoga slacks and with that starry-eyed, spaced out look that hung on me until after I'd polished off a couple of pints. I learned something from that old lady, something that may overcome my lifelong aversion to the scent of English Lavender and the sound of clacking dentures. What did I learn? I learned that sometimes, to protect yourself, you've got to set the stage a little. If you're a frail old lady, conjure up a vicious dog named Biff to keep the creeps at bay. If you're a useless, scrawny, discombobulated former university professor, take on a real job, like dealing with the great unwashed and untutored in Britain's roads, to fool people into thinking you've got the real stuff. If you are also a bit of a letdown to women, marry a voluptuous foreign woman who, if you hadn't charmed her with your posh British accent, wouldn't have given you the time of day, never mind a vow of eternal love. (By the way, to Americans—such as the lady I married most recently—any British accent is posh. If it's British, it's posh. I'm not posh. I'm from Liverpool, for crying out loud. Did the Beatles sound posh to you?)

Well, there it is. I still have some remnants of university professor in me. I occasionally use a word longer than two syllables, and foreign. And there is also that matter of the laboratory break-in. But that's another story. I had nothing to do with it, although it attempted to have something to do with me. Not unlike the current dilemma, in fact. I've got nothing to do with the current event, either, and yet it has consumed my life.

TWO

Racing in the Street

I have been a driving instructor for almost a decade now, since shortly after it became dangerous to be alone with those who might possibly be on a government watch list: Muslims, Mafia operatives, people who had protested government activities…in short, types one often finds within the crumbling corridors of ancient university buildings. But that makes it all the more interesting. The dual controls have come in useful more than once, although that one Iranian man is suing me for breaking his nose. As I've been at pains to point out, I didn't break it. The airbag broke it when it went off in response to my pounding the brakes while grabbing the wheel so we *would* hit that stone wall. Hitting the wall seemed preferable to me to being riddled in the ribs with the heat he was packing…And after the mumblings in Farsi or something when I told him he'd be ready to drive in Britain a month after all the Muslim Virgins got knocked up….Well, you can see why driving into a brick wall and breaking his nose was the better choice. As far as I know, he never even went to hospital. He probably just went home to his mates and had one of them set it with the flat of his hand. Anyway, I never saw him again, a fact that almost made me into a believer.

###

I believe that political correctness can be a form of linguistic fascism, and it sends shivers down the spine of my generation who went to war against fascism.—P. D. James

###

I'd like to say the insurance company had been as easy to deal with in the end. But the insurance company was less amused than I was. "Mr. Barker. I'm not at all sure we should pay for this," was the first thing out of the mouth of that simpering female sent by Comparethemerkins.com to "adjust" my claim. I couldn't help noticing that she was one of those daft females who paint their lips way outside the actual lip line, as if that would make them look like Angelina Jolie. This one not only lacked pouty lips; she had almost no lips at all, just a thin, compressed line where one might assume her lips, if any, would meet. Nonetheless, I had the feeling she was pretty good at talking, and I'd not like much of it.

I stared off into space. I was not thinking about how to get her to approve my claim. I was thinking about whether I could get past the lip liner and take advantage of the luscious cleavage peeking out from her silk man-tailored shirt, all bordered in lace. And then I remembered who I was. All that stuff had been knocked out of me by paying three alimonies—and the assurance from my current wife that things would go badly for me if I even thought about hanky-panky. Plus the current Biff had transferred his allegiance to her. I was now in danger from the crushing jaws of a canine conjugal relations cop if I so much as looked at my wife wrong. I didn't know how it happened. I was pretty good on assessing stuff like driving skills, but women? Please.

Did I fear my wife just because Biff was her knight in furry armour? No. I still had the padded gauntlets I had used to teach Biff to be Biff-like in the first place. Did I fear her because she was an American? Hell no. I feared her because she was an Italian-American and all her cousins and uncles had names like Rocco and "Lips" Morello and Toni "Tiger" Timpanelli. I swear. That one wasn't an uncle, though, it was an aunt. And what with all the body and facial hair, the woman did look like Tony the

Tiger, the popular cartoon promoting American breakfast cereal. I had no illusions, though. I figured "Toni" was a lot more fearsome than American breakfast cereal, and that's saying a lot.

Back in the moment, I attended to business.

"It was clearly an accident," I replied. I pulled myself up to my full height, six feet and six inches of motley flesh hung loosely on my elegantly cadaverous frame.

"It is incumbent upon driving instructors not to allow harm to befall innocent bystanders because of the lurid driving habits of some students. Since I hadn't known what he was pulling from under his jalaba or whatever they call those shroud-like garments Arab men wear, I had to get the car away from any point where it would do harm to the public."

She still looked sceptical. Apparently, she had never been in a car with a learner driver who spoke little English and seemed to bear some animus, in fact, toward not only his new adopted nation, but certain representatives thereof. Namely me.

I continued trying to get Ms. Lipless to see it my way. "Clearly it was an accident, and a far less horrific one than would have occurred had he shot me and his lack of skill sent the car out of control and into a crowd of pedestrians, for god's sake."

"Mr. Barker. There was no gun."

"But still…if there had been….."

"THERE. WAS. NO. GUN."

I hung my head. What else could I do? It was obviously time to make Ms. Compare think I was an imbecile and take pity on me. According to The Cobra (and two of the three other wives), that shouldn't be hard. And it wasn't.

"I couldn't know that, could I? I'm not a police profiler. Heck, I have a hard time remembering my name. How can I be expected to remember a whole bunch of characteristics that might mean a person is a criminal, or even a dodo? I have all I can do to keep the learners from filling the hospitals. I'm not trying to claim what I do is valuable, like saving citizens money in their insurance claims as you do. But I like to think my job serves an important function in society, and that by ruining a car, I might have saved lives."

She still wasn't convinced, despite the flattery. I could tell because her lips had disappeared even further.

"And all my student suffered was a broken nose. It probably served him as a badge of honour. He could claim he got it in the jihad."

She almost burst out laughing.

"You do have a way about you, Mr. Barker," she said. "I have absolutely no reason to approve a claim for damage done when you set off the air bags by causing an accident on purpose. However, considering the extent of your creativity in explaining why I should grant your claim for compensation, I have no choice but to authorize payment."

Nah, that's not really what she said. She narrowed her already beady little eyes, turned the lips downward until they looked more like a garrotte being prepared for use than human tissue, and issued a proclamation through clenched teeth. "I'll OK this. I have had quite enough of being put upon by foreigners moving to the UK and taking advantage of our social safety net, especially when they hate us to begin with. APPROVED!"

I was astonished. I gave myself credit for political correctness and human kindness, both of which run but thinly in my veins. And I gave her credit for being ethnocentric and chauvinistic and therefore politically incorrect as well. And I also credited her with human kindness to me. Indeed, I figured I had sucked up every molecule of human kindness she had stored for the week.

So Ms. Compare approved the payout for the car and for the wog's nose. Whew. And please excuse the ethnic slur. I'm still not my politically correct self...but don't hold your breath waiting.

Then she gave me her version of a smile; fortunately, I figured it out quickly and did not offer her a Pepto-Bismol tablet for her stomach. We ended up parting friends, although I can't say I ever wanted to see her again for any reason.

The other thing that makes this job interesting is that there are no types. No Goths (well, some Goths, but they drop out of Goth role-play, to use a term we often use to describe the corporate-speak of the government's driving examiners—
although the students who fail tend to be a bit rougher in their descriptions). No posh kids.

OK...Some posh kids. But their hoity-toity training gets pretty well ironed out when it comes to driving—one of the few endeavours guaranteed to scare the lightly caned bottoms off spoiled public school rich kids and the dirt off the elbows of shirtless poor ones alike—and they are as individual in their annoying habits, or endearing charms, as anyone else.

The driving instructor's athletes are generally known as "boy racers" and they fail their first driving test at alarming rates. They think they know it all. They think their reactions are faster than anyone else's. And then reality smacks them down, and they realize that the internal combustion engine, surrounded by garishly painted hunks of asbestos, is a great equalizer. Anyone who can reach the pedals and turn the steering wheel has just as much likelihood of being a great driver as a boy racer, maybe more. Boy racers lack the one thing good driving demands: common sense.

###
When buying a used car, punch the buttons on the radio. If all the stations are rock and roll, there's a good chance the transmission is shot.—Larry Lujack
###

A thing in short supply globally, I would say. My boss has none, for example. And therein lies the crux of my current dilemma: While John Wayne Bulpitt is a moron, I didn't really see how I could mention the recent disappearance of his wife to the police. Well, not that recent, really. She has been gone a long time, a really long time. Sufficient time, I should think, for the decomposition of the body found in the boot of the Car From 'L parked on the back lot at the driving school. It was a sort of "emergency" car. We use it only when the regular spare is undergoing routine maintenance (which happens frequently, especially with the preponderant manual shifts whose clutches are abused by gorilla feet and gear shift levers manhandled by hands that would look good on Hulk Hogan), or when one of us has a student he or she particularly wants to bedevil. Would any instructor DO such a thing?

Let me put it this way. In the UK, there is a popular TV show called *Dangerous Drivers*. One would think that a nation that requires an A performance to pass the written driving test—the theory test—and that test is based on the ENTIRE highway code, as contained in two books (one of 364 pages, one of *only* 143), anyone on the road had intellect enough to be there. There is also a hazards test that must be passed, and even some instructors failed it when it first came out. And then there's the Practical Test, 40 minutes in a car proving that one can actually carry out virtually every manoeuvre in both books, safely, calmly and with attention to every conceivable detail.

One would think. So how did the man who drives ten miles under the speed limit at all times, and thinks he's a good driver, get through a test in which one is expected to be at the speed limit at all times, road conditions permitting? It's both a traffic congestion thing and an environmental thing, the driving examiner demand that drivers get the car out of the petrol-greedy lower gears. But pass he did, this OAP wannabe, and finally was forced to take a remedial driving course by his mother (his mother!) and friends, none of whom would ride with him. His instructor, a tough young woman, almost punched him out. He disagreed with virtually everything she told him about his driving and what to do about it, and left the lesson STILL convinced he's a good, safe driver, and still driving at no more than 20 mph, regardless. Lord help us. These people are on English roadways. Morons. Not unlike Bulpitt whose ONLY saving grace is that, unaccountably, the moron can drive well. He rose to his current pinnacle of influence through the ranks. Now that I think of it, both rank and moron seem to fit Bulpitt perfectly.

The one thing that unites all human beings, regardless of age, gender, religion, economic status or ethnic background, is that, deep down inside, we ALL believe that we are above average drivers.—Dave Barry, "Things That It Took Me 50 Years to Learn"

John Wayne Bulpitt, however, likes to think his first two names exemplify his personality. He's alone in that concept. The rest of us, as far as I know, think his last name should probably be Bobbitt instead of Bulpitt. Who's Bobbitt?

Let me take you on a nostalgic journey across the sea. In June, 1993, a young married couple in Manassas, Virginia, USA, got drunk and the man got frisky. Too frisky. His wife, Lorena, later claimed he raped her because she was not interested in serving his needs. He slept soundly, apparently as only the drunk shall sleep. When Lorena went to the kitchen to seek a glass for water to slake her booze-induced thirst, she had the compelling thought that she should also obtain the sharpest knife in the drawer. That would probably have been the only sharp knife in any drawer in that house, but I digress.

Lorena returned to her sleeping husband, cut off his penis—apparently without his awakening—went to her car, drove around for a while, and tossed the salami out the window. Well, half a salami; the other half being still attached to Bobbitt, who was probably on his way to the hospital. As it happens, Lorena had seen the horror of her ways and called 911 (the US emergency number, like 999) herself and turned herself in. Whereupon police had searched the field where the salami had landed, had found it, packed it in ice, and had taken it to the surgeons who reattached it to a doubtless grateful John Wayne Bobbitt. One has to wonder if the reattachment resulted in any deformity or diminution of the crucial measurement. But one needn't wonder too long; Bobbitt has had lovers since then, and they weren't after the ne'er-do-well's wealth, that's for sure. Aside from several arrests, including one for stealing $140,000 from a clothing store in Las Vegas (of course), he worked as a bartender and tow truck operator among other things…one of those things being wedding chapel minister of a Universal Life Church in Las Vegas.

I don't make this stuff up. And yes, I am thinking about becoming a Universal Life Church minister myself. Doing so would be unlikely to interfere with any of my other life goals. The church, founded by a man disappointed in the Pentecostal

Church (you work it out; maybe he didn't know where to find any poisonous snakes…I could tell him, since I do know where The Cobra lives), vows not to interfere with a person's personal beliefs about God or religion, or just about anything.

In fact, I knew a couple of Universal Life Church ministers for a while, during my yoga days. One of them later became a telephone psychic. He liked the graveyard shift, from about midnight until 4 a.m., for two reasons. First, the pay-per-minute was higher because the company had a hard time snagging lazy bastards who would rather daydream out loud during daylight hours for a pittance than work hard for bigger pay checks at such an inconvenient hour. Second, the range of questions from the seekers of truth was more interesting.

Another one married himself to his girlfriend, although he was gay, because she was pregnant. Yes, the sprog was his. Since they had never actually reported the marriage to the civil authorities, all they did to get divorced was circle each other three times in their living room while saying, "I divorce you, I divorce you, I divorce you." Done, the way I understand Muslims can also do it. The kid, however, remains viable and is about 25 by now.

By the way, the church does have one creed: "Do only that which is right." I like that. The pedant in me appreciates NOT reading, "Do only what is right," which is wrong. But my spirit resonates with that concept, mostly. Which almost brings me to the crux of my current dilemma. I really want to get into the subject of names again, though; don't worry. The subject is germane (that will be 50p, please). It will eventually bring us back to John Wayne Bulpitt.

So…

THREE

Stop in the Name of Love

Have you ever noticed how often names seem to fit—or is it predict?—life experiences of their owners? A fiction writer couldn't come up with a better name for an egomaniacal American who fancied himself a matinee idol and who was shorn where it hurts—bobbed, you might say—than John Wayne Bobbitt.

In fact, an American wrote a whole book about that several years—quite a few years—before the Bobbitt case. John Train, author of *Remarkable Names of Real People*, offered a few, including some of my favourites, including:

- Superporn Poopattana
- T. Hee
- Ima Hogg (Texas philanthropist)
- Doctor Daniel Doctor (a real eye doctor in Westport, Connecticut)
- Minnie Magazine (really, truly, the late cable desk editor of Time, Inc., publications)

I had a friend at university who had a cousin named Allen Katz....nicknamed Allie, of course.

And then there was Miracle Johnson. The name isn't bad by itself. And I taught Miss Miracle Johnson to drive one year. A year later, I again saw the name Miracle Johnson on my list of the week's students. What had happened, I wondered. Had she done some really bad driving and racked up more than six points, meaning she'd need to pass her test all over again to continue driving? I was dying to find out, but I didn't see her among the gaggle of students all seeking their instructors in the Cars From 'L car park. There was a young woman who looked like her, quite a bit. And she was the only one left standing when the rest had joined their instructors.

"I guess they must have mixed you up with a student from last year," I said, greeting her.

"No, I'm Miracle Johnson."

I stood there looking a lot like some of my lesser students, jaw slack, vacant look in my eyes. "Umm….."

"It's OK. Most people can't figure it out. My mother had a hard time conceiving, so when my sister was born, she decided it was a miracle. She never thought she'd be able to have a second child, so that was a miracle, too. She didn't want to insult fate by naming me anything else."

"Ah."

As it turned out, I never lost touch with Miracle Johnson, the second Miracle Johnson. She liked the driving school so much, she applied for the job of receptionist and was hired by Bulpitt, who, unaccountably, had a soft spot in his heart for her. She never did pass her driving test. She decided taking the bus to work was fine, no doubt because it gave her more time to work on her accents.

###

Miracles occur naturally as expressions of love. The real miracle is the love that inspires them. In this sense everything that comes from love is a miracle. —Marianne Williamson

###

"Nice-a day, Mistera Barker," she said to me this morning. "I'ma gonna make-a you a nice-a cuppa 'spresso."

"Yes, thanks," I said, not really wanting a cup of espresso. Riding with this week's students looked to be nerve-wracking enough. But I didn't want to push any of Miracle's buttons. It's dangerous. She holds the keys to the spare learner cars, so she can, if she wants, make your life miserable when your regular car is in for servicing. Particularly this week, since she was into Mafia-speak, I didn't want to annoy her. For all I knew, she was taking lessons. Maybe from an actual Italian, considering Miracle was pretty good at that accent and could keep it up for quite a while.

She did much less well with her month of the Finnish tongue...not that many people know what pidgin Finnish sounds like. How many Finns are there? Funny you should ask...so I looked it up. Only a little over five million. It would be tough to hear Finnish outside Finland. It's similar to Estonian, though, and related to Hungarian, which sounds very different. How do I know this? Recall, I was a professor. *I looked it up.* You thought professors just KNEW all that stuff? Hah. Mainly, we are really good at looking stuff up. Anyway, Finnish is one of the Fenno-Ugric languages, which also claims some languages spoken in Russia by infinitesimally small ethnic groups. The famous "they" think that Fenno-Ugric languages might be related to Indo-European languages (English,, German, Latin, etc.), but "they" admit it is highly debatable.

Maybe Miracle was taking Italian accent lessons from my wife. Nah. Not a chance. My wife doesn't speak like that. As she is fond of telling people, when they hear that her original surname was Corleone—I swear—some Italians do believe in education and learn to speak proper English. OK. She says "proper English": I always add "proper American English," and that always gets me a fine Italian phrase in return, a sneer and sometimes a familiar hand gesture. They don't wring all of the ethnicity out of them at that posh Connecticut boarding school the godfa....I mean, her Uncle, Big Rosie, sent her to.

Also, my wife doesn't like Miracle.

"Whatsa matta? You doh-na like-a my café?" Miracle asked when I didn't immediately burn my lips on the tiny cup she set before me on the desk we all used, from time to time, for paperwork. I was doing some paperwork this morning.

"The coffee is fine, Miracle," I told her. "Thanks." And put my head back down and peered at the week's roster. Not sufficient. She didn't take the hint. She was hanging behind my chair like a coat.

"You know, I gotta big-a problem," she said. "I thinka Mistera Bul-a-peet he's a like-a me more than, you know, he's-a shoulda like an employee. I meana, his-a wife, she's-a missing...."

It was true. But to my knowledge, that was the sort of thing we would keep from Miracle; even Bulpitt would keep that from Miracle. Would she blab it all over town? Let's put it this way: When one of the instructors was done for drink-driving, that information suddenly appeared in *The Daily Mail*. Sure, those records are accessible to the public. But why would *The Daily Mail* care about an obscure driving instructor in an obscure city? There are prime ministers to bedevil, and no lack of ammunition for those rumour mills, either. And captains of industry. And of course, there is the ever-popular Socialist witch hunt and the mandate that every paper, and particularly tabloid types, give Tony Benn some ink from time to time. So why a nobody from Cars From 'L? My opinion is that Miracle is looking for a miracle, a fast train out of nowhere. That's not how I think of my beloved city, but my supposition regarding Miracle's thoughts. But perhaps she'd like to move to, say, Hollywood where she won't ever have to learn to drive because her chauffeur, after she becomes a famous Italian-American actress like.....like....Lady Gaga. Lady Gaga's real name is Stefani Joanne Angelina Germanotta.

Most things in life are moments of pleasure and a lifetime of embarrassment; photography is a moment of embarrassment and a lifetime of pleasure.—Tony Benn

Or if Miracle does want to drive, getting a US licence is so much easier, even Miracle could do it. She still has no idea that traffic on roundabouts all goes in one direction, but in the US, there are very few roundabouts. She could easily drive for years without encountering one, unless she has the bad luck to find herself in Washington, D.C., a city of circles—and not in traffic layout only. It is the capital of the US. Enough said. As for England's roundabouts, "It's the lanes that confuse me, Mr. Barker," she told me at the time. "And the fact that cars can enter from anywhere." She wasn't using accents back then. And no matter how many times I told her, and even showed her, that traffic in roundabouts all went the same way, she was convinced she would have a head-on collision "with all those cars and even lorries just dashing in and out any old way," she told me once, pulling up to the central reservation of a roundabout and stopping. Just stopping. With traffic whizzing by or squealing brakes behind her, and offering the full range of British creativity with linguistic aggression.

"No, not anywhere. Only where there's an entrance," I assured her. To no avail. It is, as I said, just as well that she likes taking the bus. What's really frightening is that she now has an iPad. If she were driving, she couldn't access it at least while she was behind the wheel. But I fear she will find the website of *The Speech Accent Archive* since she has a couple of hours on the bus each day and nothing else to do. It's a wacky website, despite being supported by George Mason University, one of the better-thought-of US institutions of higher learning. As such, it naturally offers intense, in-depth information on the subject of accents. It is not inconceivable that Miracle will someday discover more than the Italian, French, German, Spanish and Dracula accents she has affected and all-but-perfected to date. I imagine she could handle bambara, an accent from Mali, or maybe Romanian, although that is fairly close to the Dracula she has been working on.

She might even perfect the speech of immigrants living in the US or Canada and speaking English, or people from either of those nations moving to the UK and attempting to speak actual English. All that information is provided on the sample used by the academics to compare the pronunciation of various non-native English speakers. They all read the same passage:

> Please call Stella. Ask her to bring these things with her from the store: Six spoons of fresh snow peas, five thick slabs of blue cheese, and maybe a snack for her brother Bob. We also need a small plastic snake and a big toy frog for the kids. She can scoop these things into three red bags, and we will go meet her Wednesday at the train station.

You can look it up on the www.accent.gmu.edu website. Or you can wait with me for Miracle to begin talking about snow peas and plastic snakes—maybe snah piss ant plestik steks if she's in a Russian mood—although the juxtaposition of those two things in conversation might not be thought that weird for a woman whose hair, at any given moment, is a combination of brown, soylent green, fuchsia and blue.

The website offers more accents even than Miracle has piercings (I think she's up to about ten now, fortunately most on some portion of one of her ears. At least the ones I know of.) Even I have never heard of some of the languages. Babur? Bouole? Fataluku? Tok pisin? (!*&&^%!)

As it happens, tok pisin is a dialectical speech pattern from Papua, New Guinea. If memory serves, that's the very place author Alexander McCall Smith writes about when he retells the story of a visit to that island by Prince Charles, and the way his host introduced him as, "Numba one pickaninny bilong Mrs. Kwin."

Despite Miracle's obvious departures from what anyone might desire in a receptionist for a famous driving school, Bulpitt is fond of her. As noted, she seems to think he's more than fond of her. But at least, he doesn't seem to loathe her as he loathes everyone else. All right, not everyone. I meant as he loathes me.

I've never figured it out. My students have a good pass rate. My time is always booked. And I don't complain too much about the garish appearance of the Cars From 'L. To be fair, every learner driver in Britain drives a car with a fairly large red L stuck on it, front and rear. When mum and dad teach Junior to drive, they buy the plastic magnetized things and put them on the car where they can be easily seen. The Ls are supposed to come off when Junior is not driving, but no one bothers, and apparently the cops don't either. It would not go well, though, for a learner to be caught behind the wheel of an L-less car.

So maybe that's the reason Cars From 'L is so overboard with its signage. Many companies simply put tasteful Ls on the front and rear and attach a sort of taxi-sign to the top with the company's name and phone number on it. But not Cars From 'L. Oh, no. Cars From 'L come in many colours, as long as those colours are electric blue, bright red, neon green or orange. Then Cars From 'L is painted on the bonnet slanting form driver's to passenger's side. A similar, if slightly smaller, logo is printed on each side, and on the back. In addition, front and rear, in the space not used for the Cars From 'L logo, there is a big red L at least three times the size of the Ls mom and pop can buy. Good advertising? Sure. But garish.

Why do I care? I'm a tasteful sort of guy. I felt lucky, when I married my wife, that she had gone to prep school and learned how to be what the Americans call a WASP, White Anglo-Saxon Protestant, instead of her natural White Sicilian Roman Catholic, which doesn't even have a recognized acronym. Plus, the garden variety WSRC usually has taste that extends to a houseful of cheap capo di monte tchotchkes serving no useful purpose (as opposed to the antique, lovely and collectible examples), lime green carpets, and white satin furniture covered permanently in clear plastic zip covers lest they get marred when used. How do I know this? My wife explained it all to me when we were courting, in case I would reject her on the basis of a cultural preference for garish décor.

By the way, just so you know, my vocabulary has grown considerably since I met my wife. Anyone who grows up in New York City, the world's melting pot, learns not only their own ethnic slang, but the ethnic slang of other cultures they are rubbing shoulder with 24/7. Tchotchkes is a Yiddish word meaning small (annoying) useless objects, the sort of thing you find in your old Gran's house, since she has doubtless reached the age where moving all that crap around and dusting it constitutes the sum total of the week's excitement.

###

"The chances of overhearing a conversation in Vlashki, a variant of Istro-Romanian, are greater in Queens [a borough of New York City] than in the remote mountain villages in Croatia that immigrants now living in New York left years ago."— "Listening to (and Saving) the World's Languages," *New York Times*, **April 29, 2010, p. A1**

###

I realize all this sounds horribly bigoted or maybe even ageist, but it isn't. It is simple fact. Old folks don't work, so they dust. And Brits like matte finishes, fine porcelain used for things like eating, paintings with a minimum of flying winged babies, etc. On the other hand, British food is boring in the extreme. I would almost trade a calm interior for the much more exciting cuisine of the sunny south of Sicily. But I didn't have to. My wife—when she deigned to cook—offered me the best of both worlds. Terrific cuisine. One night, she made peposo.

"What are you cooking?" I called when I entered. The smell was wonderful, meaty and spicy. But not Indian. Hmmm..

"Peposo," she said.

"Pepto...."

"No. Pep-o-so. It's a medieval beef dish that was served to men working on the roofs of cathedrals. They set it on the fire when they went up to the top, and hours later, bowls were sent up to them so they didn't have to come down."

"Oh. Well." This stuff never impressed me. It was the eating I was after.

"It has loads of black pepper, and it has been cooking all afternoon," she said. "Slow cooking, red wine and voilá. You've got peposo. You'll love it."

She was right, I did love it. It had everything that appeals to the manly British heart—good tender beef, red wine. It is served ladled over a hunk of Tuscan bread. OK. So it wasn't potatoes, which we manly Brits also love. But bread is good. More than acceptable.

"Al-Hamdolillah," I said after I burped.

"Shelf."

"OK." I liked the Arabic phrase. It means Thank God. I learned it from the guy whose nose I broke. When the ambulance arrived that day, I pointed out to him that he was hardly hurt at all. I *emphasised* that he was hardly hurt at all. That he would be back in my learner car in no time. And then I said "Al-Hamdolillah." I figured that would please him.

Through his nose, he managed to get out, "But if you are booked, then I can have another instructor? When I return?"

"Yes, of course."

"Al-Hamdolillah."

And back at ya, I thought.

Allah is on our side. That is why we will beat the aggressor.—Saddam Hussein

As for the disappearing Mrs. Bulpitt, maybe Bulpitt himself told Miracle she had gone missing. Either way, we had the local constabulary opening the boot of a car at the back of the lot. It turned out that they had been called because some neighbours had noticed a veritable river of liquid dripping from beneath and running down his driveway, which gave onto the Cars From 'L car park. Perhaps it was wishful thinking that Mrs. Bulpitt was missing and in one of the L cars.

***

There were two large black plastic bags in the thing; I could see that from the second storey window I was looking out of. No sooner had the lid popped open, though, than the two cops and the neighbour jumped back like they'd seen Lady Gaga inside, naked. Or no, maybe Dame Edna. Naked. As? Umm...well, whoever he or she is.

It wasn't long before I closed the window; a ripe odour was wafting my way. Indeed, it made me want to make a trip to a loo to puke up my guts. But I didn't. How would that look, with John Wayne Bulpitt running down the hall calling my name? He might think I had something to do with the awful stench from the car boot. What could that stench be?

I had smelt some skunk odours on a visit to the New World once. That smell was close. But not that close. What about a load of barf? Farm smells: did it smell like aged cowshit? No, not quite. Sickly.

Enough. I had to go. I didn't, thank goodness, have to go to the car park to get my vehicle. I had sneaked it into one of the executive spaces in front of the building. There was nothing left to do but go home, and rest up for another day of teaching the great unwashed to become less dangerous on England's roadways.

FOUR

Bewitched, Bothered and Bewildered

I didn't actually get home, not that night and not the next, either. On my way to my car, one of the students ran up and stopped me. "Mr. Barker," he said.

"Professor Barker," I replied. I got the usual quizzical look. OK, my doctorate means nothing at the moment, but I worked for it, I earned it, and I simply like hearing it as part of my name. And I may go back to university teaching someday, as soon as I figure no one will mention the laboratory incident. Is there a statute of limitations on dumb? Or maybe I'll just become an online teacher at the University of Internet Pursuits or something. Online learning seems to be all the rage in the colonies, and if being a professor is a licence to spend no more than 20 hours a week actually working, imagine what could be done with the interface of the internet? One need never even see, hear or smell a live student. You would think anyone who knew he or she would be spending an hour or two at close quarters with a stranger might apply a little stench-abatement lotion, wouldn't you? You'd be wrong much of the time. Ditto for toothpaste.

However, to return to the point. I never got home that night because Student Dopey, on a mission from the peelers, said I was wanted in the car park. I didn't want to go, not least because my wife had planned a great dinner that night, something she rarely does. She's an American, remember, and she had told me when we first met that what she generally made for dinner was a booking at a fine restaurant. Tonight, though, I had been promised all sorts of homemade delights. All sorts. Plus food.

I didn't want to go because of the smell. It was worse than maggoty meat; I had smelled that years ago behind a house I rented. The former tenant had thrown some meat away, just plonked it in the bin. It was a hot summer. Nature took its course and by the time I moved in, a maggoty mass filled the bottom of that bin, a bin that—I hate to admit—got fly tipped one night. To be fair, I had broken the lid off it so it couldn't close, and I chucked it out in the marshes, thinking the contents might become food for an alligator or something. Sure, I know England doesn't have alligators. It doesn't even have raccoons. But surely something lived in or near the marshes that would want to eat maggoty meat. Badgers? They couldn't be as friendly and harmless as they were written in *The Wind in the Willows*.

Most of the monsters…are based on some sort of mythology. Every culture and even some geographical areas have monsters and mythology that is their own.—Laurell K. Hamilton

I had taken the precaution of wearing gloves when I handled the rubbish bin. And I had not put anything of mine—old letters and that sort of thing—into it, ever. So it was untraceable.

I did go downstairs, though, and out to the car park as bidden by Student Dopey. Before I knew it, John Wayne Bulpitt's wife had been found. It might have been an answer to someone's prayers, but not mine. A letter addressed to me had been found under the big, black plastic bag that held the mortal remains of Gertrude Hermione Dorcas Bulpitt.

What wasn't known, though, was who the second bag contained. It was a man, probably. Mrs. Bulpitt was a big woman, but the second bag was even bigger.

It didn't seem to me that there could be any reason to question me; after all, I certainly wasn't her lover or I would have been the other body, it seems to me. If I were the other man, why would I kill the other man, even if it was *another* other man? It seemed to me that John Wayne Bulpitt was the obvious suspect. But then, his mail was not under the body. Bulpitt, always the voyeur, had run down to the car park as soon as the first peelers arrived, had stood over the car, and now that the boot had been opened, was spilling his crocodile tears into it, over the bag containing what appeared to be the mortal remains of Gertrude Hermione Dorcas Bulpitt. I admit, that isn't—wasn't—really her name, but that's what she looked like. I think her name was simply Susan.

You may be wondering, too, how they could have concluded at such an early date that the bagged body was Mrs. Bulpitt, and yet had no idea who the other stiff (although they were more like mushies) was. Simple: Bulpitt had identified a diamond necklace that had fallen out of the bag through a tear made by a...mouse? the killer?...as belonging to Mrs. B.

Where did the Bulpitts get the kind of money to buy a little bit of bling like that big bit of bling? As for how it got off Mrs. B and into the pits of the L car, that, too, was a mystery. Maybe it got caught on the boot's latch on the way in...who knows? All I know is that, before I knew it, I was experiencing the head-shove down into the back seat of a police car, just like they do it on *Law and Order*, the hit show from the US running 24/7 on British telly. Like a common criminal, I was being taken to the police station by the local constabulary to be questioned.

***

Why it should take them from 5 p.m. until midnight to question a witness is beyond me. Well, OK. So they snagged me as a potential perpetrator, based on Bulpitt's hollering and the letter bearing my name. By dawn, though, they knew I wasn't anything like a suspect. First, none of my fingerprints were on that envelope, which told them I had—as I claimed—never seen it before in my life. Second, Bulpitt's own story was unravelling at an alarming rate. After screeching that I was his wife's lover—oh, please. I do really like my romantic conquests to share a species with me, and Gertrude Hermione Dorcas Bulpitt was questionable in that regard.

I'm not going to do it. I'm not going to say, "May God strike me dead for being so mean." The woman was a hulking, vicious, massively unattractive example of what genes can do, even in a civilized nation like Great Britain. The Neander Valley may well be on the continent, but some of those genes, and the hairy arms to go with them, definitely leaped from Cherbourg to Dover at some point, and all of them conspired with the parents of Gertrude Hermione Dorcas Bulpitt to make a creature more massively unattractive even than Kerry Katona or that chunky blonde wench from The East Enders. That one who orders some fast food and makes it sound like she got a tongue depressor caught between her massive jaws last time she did a doctor a personal favour.

The ride to the police station was the most interesting thing that happened until the envelope came back without my fingerprints on it. One would think cops—the same folks who issue tickets for mistakes on the roadways—could drive better. I could have told them a few things about being in the proper lane when negotiating roundabouts, but I didn't think they'd listen. They were too busy wondering what their wives were going to cook them for dinner. Well, OK. One of them was a female member of the constabulary and she didn't seem to care about cooking at all. I just decided to make them both male because it would continue to enhance the reputation as a hard-living, reckless tosser I've been developing for you. Actually, the female copper was rather fetching. I couldn't imagine her, or any woman for that matter, in those Keystone Cops pointy helmets they used to wear. But the cap with the chequered border was cute. And the uniform, ugly black shoes and all, didn't look half bad on her. Maybe it was the dayglo green safety vest that made her boobs look humongous…or maybe the huge innocent blue eyes, or the severely pulled back auburn hair that showed off her elegant neck and nose…

It seems as if I was on the verge of a pseudo-erotic experience right there in the back of the lockup on wheels. But the truth is, I was terrified. Middle-class people, and especially former professors and yoga instructors, DO NOT go to jail.

Former dog walkers…maybe. I mean, can you think of a better excuse for someone of loose morals to legitimately have keys to and the run of a bunch of houses owned by obviously decently paid people who would have decent amounts of stuff to steal and fence for a fix? I can't. The more I think about it, the more I wonder how many dog walkers are addicts and how many steal from Fido's owners to support their cravings. It might be a good study, I thought. But not for me. All that ivory tower nonsense was behind me. I might once have been a world-class social anthropologist….I might have. But I wasn't. Just an ordinary bloke, educated beyond where it is wise to educate a member of the proletariat, trying to make a living.

An educated man is thoroughly inoculated against humbug, thinks for himself and tries to give his thoughts, in speech or on paper, some style.—Alan K. Simpson

I wasn't really worried. I had no clue as to how a letter addressed to me got into that car, but I wouldn't have put it past Bulpitt to have planted it there. Still, it's a highly unpleasant experience to be grilled by the boys and girls in blue, right up there with pissing the sheets a bit after a long night of drink when you're staying at a friend's house for the weekend. Or having a note from the Inland Revenue that you might not have done the math quite right and they want to come by and take a look at the swimming pool you deducted because your doctor friend said a nightly swim would take the edge off the cramped muscles sitting in a car all day produced...now that you weren't working out in the yoga studio anymore.

I might have pondered what the cops might have pondered. Who was the female decedent in the car? The male? Why were they dead? And why were they there? If Stiff One was Gertrude Hermione Dorcas Bulpitt, who was Stiff Two? I might have done. But my musings were far closer to home. I wondered if I had spent some time with the vics (cop talk, US TV shows) unwittingly when I had taken my last student for his practical driving test. Could they have been in the boot then? Did I recall any particular drag on the tiny engine of that rundown hulk? Any odours?

An educated person is one who has learned that information almost always turns out to be at best incomplete and very often false, misleading, fictitious, mendacious - just dead wrong.— Russell Baker

Most students who had the misfortune to drive that car never wanted to see it again. And that was well before anyone knew it was a death-mobile, obviously. But unaccountably, though, one of my students wanted to use that car, said it reminded him of the cars in his home country. He was a fairly recent immigrant, although he had to have been in the country at least six months. Immigrants can't even sign up for the theory test—a 50-question computerized quiz followed by several clips, like an arcade game, on which applicants must identify developing road hazards—until they've been in the UK at least 181 days. They have another similar time frame in which to pass both tests, since they've got to get legal with a UK licence within a year, or forget driving amongst the boy racers and, worse, the old-age pensioners who got licences *sans* testing during WWII and are still wearing down the tarmac. Slowly. Bloody slowly. They haven't forgotten the rules of the road, exactly. They never knew them, so you can't blame them. Besides, today's cars have more knobs and buttons and levers than all their medical assistive devices put together, so you have to excuse them for putting on the emergency flashers every now and then when they appear to be wanting to make a right turn.

"And luckily, therefore the good old days return. The traditional art of driving counts again, and it is all about good tactics, skills and reflexes instead of simple power."—Jacky Ickx, Belgian racing driver

At least the OAPs do most of their driving on Thursdays, so you can plan your life around it. The pension checks don't all arrive on Thursday anymore, so I'm told, but they did for a long time, and the old farts got used to doing their weekly shop on Thursday. Damn, a trip to Waitrose on Thor's special day is more like a visit to a bustling OAP care home. I don't like doing it, but sometimes, you just need a cup of coffee and Waitrose's café coffee isn't bad, and you don't have to deal with downtown parking like at Costa or Starbucks. But you do have to watch out for the old farts in the car park, a seeming mystery to most of them, all backing into the bay (yow) and then pulling halfway out into the roadway when they realize they can't get the groceries into the boot because Methuselah II has kissed their rear bumper with his rear bumper when he backed in. Of course, you can't really blame the old farts. They do what they can.

You can blame the politicians, dead politicians, who didn't see the wisdom of testing driving applicants when Der Fuhrer was dropping ordnance night after night. But they also lacked the foresight to project that having those untested drivers on the roads as they came into their Alzheimer's years would be a truly frightful idea. Sigh. Retesting them is one idea, but not one I'm personally fond of. Some unlucky instructors would have to serve their needs. The immigrants are bad enough.

We get a lot of immigrants at Cars From 'L. The student who wanted to use the "death car" was from some African state, some state that doesn't have the same name it did when I studied geography at age 12. About the only ones I know anymore are South Africa and Mali. I don't know why I know Mali. South Africa is obvious. First, it is descriptive. Second, the UK used to own it.

The student who wanted to use the car that was really from 'ell wasn't much to write home about, except for that.

I had had a previous African student, though, who still deserves some ink from me, and probably, if my imagination is not getting away from me, from more than one global police department. That student was...umm...tribal. Not banging drums/painting bodies tribal. The OTHER tribal...organized crime tribal. Well, I don't actually know that, but I'll give you a few facts so you can figure out what you think. Actually, it might be worse than organized crime, especially post 9/11.

Still, the facts are the facts about my Central African Disaster, who might well have appropriated the moniker Captain Africa, such was his belief in his prowess and ability to drive after only a week of wildly interrupted lessons. (Since he would have liked being called that, and he's high on my lifetime list of Who Not To Piss Off, I'll use it. If his relatives ever see this, they'll think well of me. I hope.)

Where in Central Africa he came from, I cannot recall, if I ever knew. Uganda? Maybe. Uganda was a former British colony, cobbled together before independence from a bunch of often warring tribes, and led—if you can call it that—by the monstrous Idi Amin from 1971 to 1979, when he scarpered. OK. He was deposed, first lodging as a guest of his Libyan whack job counterpart, Kaddafi, and then moving on to Saudi Arabia as a guest of the Saudi royal family—a guest who was given a huge stipend for promising the Saudis that he would stay out of politics.

Anyway, the point is that Ugandans are likely to speak pretty good English, considering its status as a former colony. And the other thing, something that got to me the closer I got to Captain Africa, was this: Amin had between six and thirteen wives depending on whose figures you prefer, fathered untold children (scary, since he was apparently syphilitic), and not all of them were, you should excuse the term, lily white.

His son Faisal Wangita, born in 1983 after Amin was living in exile, was convicted and sent to jail for five years in 2007 for beating to death an 18-year-old at the Camden tube station. The charge? Conspiracy to wound with intent and violent disorder. In short, he's his father's son.

I'm not suggesting that my African student was this man; first, the dates don't work. And it seems unlikely that offspring of Idi Amin would be taking driving lessons in a medium-sized city; wouldn't such offspring just force someone to drive them around, or maybe squander some of the loot Amin collected while in power or as a guest of an oil-rich nation and left to them after a highly publicized inheritance squabble? Probably. No need for lessons when one has a driver. Although this Wangita character seems to have been a penniless git.

No matter. I seriously doubt my student was related to the monstrous Idi Amin. After all, we were alone in a small car for hours, and if he had wanted to hurt me because he couldn't drive and wanted to make it my fault as any self-respecting psychopath would do...who was to stop him? A mild-mannered ex-professor and former yoga instructor? Probably not.

"You know, I am a landlord in your country. I have several magnificent properties in my portfolio," Captain Africa told me early on. Actually, he declaimed it, in a voice and accent reminiscent of Eddie Murphy's portrayal of Prince Akeem in that iconic movie, *Coming to America*. So it wasn't too weird that he had two mobile phones with him. When they rang, invariably he would pull over to the side of the road.

"You will kindly excuse me, Mr. Barker? My business has immediate need of my attention. I shall not be long. We will continue with our lesson very shortly." Prince Akeem, in suburban England.

When he returned to the car, it was always the same.

"It was a favorite tenant who is having trouble with his plumbing," he would say.

Or sometimes, something like ,"My insurance agent has rung up and told my assistant he is in need of additional premium immediately, so I will have to—so unfortunately—end our lesson early." Then he would drive us back to the Cars From 'L building, and his limo would pick him up.

I never knew for sure what, if anything, was true. He walked so far from the car for his conversations that although I did my best to listen while not appearing to listen, I heard nothing. Not a thing. Odd, from the booming timbre of his voice when he was assuring me that I was indeed the greatest teacher he had ever known.

At the time, I figured it was drugs he was discussing. But then, since each break took about ten minutes, that seemed a stretch after a while. I mean, how long does it take to say, "No, that figure is insufficient. You will need to put £100,000 in a plain briefcase and deliver it this evening at 9 if you want the merchandise." Plus, in the mirrors, I could see him gesticulating wildly, as if he were trying to explain quantum physics to Kerry Katona and getting nowhere.

Could he have been into prostitution? Maybe he was a pimp. But how long would it take—and how often would calls need to be taken?—to make sure his stable was toeing the line? And who would call him on his mobile, anyway? One of the girls to say she hoped he'd get back soon so he could beat her?

And then I thought maybe he was involved with some sort of terrorist outfit. OK. That was scary. It would explain why he paid for every lesson with a wad of notes he pulled from a briefcase that always accompanied him to lessons. Of course, the other two possibilities explained that nicely, too. Still, I wondered. And worse, I wondered how long I was going to have to wonder. Considering that he drove for no more than 30 minutes of any hour, his progress as a driver was almost non-existent. But he wanted, at one point, to take the test anyway. I couldn't dissuade him. He insisted in tones worthy of James Earl Jones, that he would take his test on Friday.

"Well, we can't guarantee that," I said.

He scowled at me.

"We have to call the Test Centre to see when the next available slot is open. Give me a couple of days and times that are preferable for you, and I will ask our scheduler to try very hard to book a test then."

"That is not acceptable, Shelf," he said. Ah. He usually called me Mr. Barker. He was trying to position me in a way to ensure I did his bidding, that I was not his equal. Well, it wouldn't work.

Let me be clear: It would have worked with *ME*. I'm a sorry, whimpering tool, as they say in America. But it wouldn't work with Her Majesty's Test Centres, period. They did what they did how they did it, and the best we could do was employ a woman full-time to keep pestering them for slots and cancellations to accommodate our students.

"I cannot do anything about it. You understand, we are dealing not with people but with government employees."

He considered a moment, then nodded sagely.

"Ah, I understand. Well, do your best."

He looked at his calendar and told me what days and times would be acceptable.

I did get a test booked for him. However, although I am a nice guy, I am not stupid. I didn't take him to the test centre I usually use, where people know me. (Chicken shit. Go ahead. Say it.) I took him to one out of town. Where, of course, he failed miserably.

On the way to the test centre I had to stop him to warn him that his driving was so bad that if it didn't improve instantly, he was in danger of the test being abandoned by the examiner who had the responsibility for saving his or her own life in regard of future service to the Crown and the safety of its roadways.

Sure enough, 20 minutes into the test I saw the examiner walking back to the test centre. He explained that my student's driving was so poor that he had to stop the test for everyone's safety!

The examiner gave me directions to where he had left my car, the African student still behind the wheel but under strict instructions not to drive it under any circumstances. Not to escape an approaching fire, not even to escape a tsunami.

I trudged off and found Captain Africa staring at his green Fail sheet. In less than twenty minutes, he had achieved 19 minor faults, four serious faults and two dangerous ones.

Astonishingly, he was not upset. "Do not worry, Mr. Barker" he said. "I am going home on Monday and there I will buy a licence." Well, at least I had been returned to my pedestal and was Mr. Barker again.

As for the licence, of course he would buy one. But what did he mean by home? I'm certain, if he came from Uganda, he could manage to hook up with the remaining criminal elements and buy a licence, but that wouldn't do him much good in England, although—shudder—he could drive on it as a guest for a full year before needing to have obtained a UK licence.

While there are several websites offering fake UK licences, using one is not a good idea. Even for African princes. Doing so could mean ten years' imprisonment. Driving without any licence isn't as bad, only 3-6 penalty points and up to a £1,000 fine and possible disqualification and possible seizure of vehicle.—Researched by Prof. G. Barker

###

It crossed my mind more than once that he was from the Central African Republic, another diamond hot spot. Perhaps he was involved in getting diamonds out, in stolen diamonds. Not blood diamonds, exactly, like Sierra Leone's product. But as it happens, the Central African Republic does have very lax export controls, and a diamond production industry that leaves a lot of room for small, bright, shiny things to go missing. Rather than mines, the diamonds in the CAR are near the surface, ready to be found by anyone with rudimentary tools—shovels, picks, buckets. There is bloodshed over it all, to be sure, but not quite the grisly sort in Sierra Leone, as far as I knew. I didn't dare ask Abidemi about that.

OK. His first name was Abidemi. It just slipped out. But I had looked it up. It means "born in the father's absence." Apparently, that is a notable condition in Africa; it's not much less notable in the UK, these days. I think we used to call them bastards, but political correctness has killed that useful term off, too. Or maybe it simply meant that daddy was out hunting endangered species when the stork arrived, not that he had done a bunk to avoid daddyhood. How would I know? I'm not a cultural historian nor a linguist nor a student of African tribal customs, at least not beyond being totally enamored of all the modern music born in the syncopation of African musicians with the Caribbean. (I put this in not just to tell you how much I enjoy the music of the late Bob Marley, but also Harry Belafonte. I put it in so you'll know that despite my unfortunate mouth and despicable habit of being completely non-PC, I really do love and admire all world cultures and peoples.

Except those rat bastards from the fundamentalist heartland of America. The ones who demonstrate at the funerals of young men sacrificed in useless wars, and who want to regulate what adult women can or cannot do with their bodies, and even decide what sort of sexuality adult humans are allowed to enjoy. I loathe those rat bastards, and fortunately they have not yet become protected by law, not even in that squirrel cage known as the American Congress.)

The aforementioned rat bastards should never be confused with the quite respectable Rat Bastard Protective Association. This was a group of Beat and Funk artists who worked, lived and exhibited in San Francisco, CA, US from the late 50s to mid-60s.—Researched by Prof. G. Barker

###

I had mentioned the possible diamond connection during a rare hour out of the car, swilling Bulpitt's bad coffee with colleagues.

"What I want to know," I mused, "is where Captain Africa gets his money."

"Could be drugs," someone said.

"Or prostitutes."

"Or diamonds. Maybe he's smuggling diamonds. Wouldn't you smuggle diamonds into England and then drive them over to the continent to be cut?" someone else piped up.

The only silent one, as we made a game out of Capt. Africa's Loot, was Ignatz. He wasn't usually that quiet. Don't think it was his accent, either, because he has virtually none. He couldn't teach if he did, young Brits being less than great linguists. I hadn't spent much time with Ignatz, but in the infrequent staff meetings, he had always contributed, and usually something valuable or amusing. Come to think of it, though, he had sent an excuse for missing the most recent staff meeting. And I thought he had seemed a little quieter than usual lately. Maybe he was ill.

Maybe he missed his homeland. I had heard something about a sick mother he was flying out to visit fairly often.

Or Captain Africa might have meant he was going to whatever county in the UK he now considered home to buy a licence; he was enrolled in the week-long intensive program so there was no telling where he might have come from to book in for the week. Bulpitt doesn't grill people about why they want an intensive course, or why they want to book into the fleabag hotel that keeps rooms for us. He only grills them about their credit card numbers, which is as it should be, I suppose, this country having become increasingly capitalist during the Labour government. Don't ask. If I get into politics, I'll never finish the story of the two body bags, or my transition from my position as driving instructor in a reasonably large English city to my next incarnation. What's that? Well, you've seen how it is. You can't expect me to be a driving instructor forever, can you? Look at the list of jobs I've already racked up. Besides, Biff was getting bored at home with my wife. I needed a job where I could take him along, and he did tend to intimidate driving students who were nervous enough already.

Still, I liked being a driving instructor, and gave serious consideration to every aspect of the job. Possibly, I thought later, I should have warned the unsuspecting British public about Abidemi—Captain Africa—but how? And he's not likely to be the worst thing on our roads, either. There's a woman someplace in England who finally passed her driving test after something like 650 tries. The odds that she would finally get a simple test route and an incredibly forgiving examiner finally worked out in her favour, although I'm not certain that's in the best interests of the British population. But I'm only one man, after all, and I have no favours due from the likes of Rupert Murdoch to place advertising about the truly dangerous driver-wannabes on the roads. Anyway, it would seem that as horrible as Captain Africa was, the lady who took 650 tries before the Driving Fairy alighted upon her had to be at least as bad. I think Abidemi could have passed it, based on luck and the practice he'd get before subsequent tests were abandoned early by the examiner, in under 500 tries. Maybe even under 400.

I did mull the ethical aspects of allowing Abidemi to escape my grasp unschooled. But that didn't worry Bulpitt in the least. He was making noises as if it did. But I knew Bulpitt. He wasn't worried about Captain Africa, nor the great British road-using public. He was worried about future tuition for the school.

"What if Captain Africa bad-mouths us?" Bulpitt wondered.

"I'm more worried if he doesn't," I replied. "People are a lot like their friends; do you want many more like him on board?"

Bulpitt inadvertently rubbed his thumb across his forefinger, the universal sign for acquisitiveness. "No one says you'd get them all. You could possibly talk me into assigning them to a different instructor."

I laughed. Snorted, actually. Bulpitt frowned.

"First, how are we going to know which of the potential mortal dangers are his friends? Second, how am I going to either earn enough money to bribe you, or find it in the depths of my heart to pretend I like you and ask you nicely not to assign them to me?"

Bulpitt ignored all of that.

"Why didn't you switch him to an automatic?" Bulpitt uselessly suggested, as if absent a clutch the student could have performed better, what with the inattentiveness and truncated lessons. I gave him a look.

"Well, then, you really should not have taken him for a test; how will that look, the school taking him for a test when he was so far from ready?"

Indeed. I had no really good answer to that one, except that he paid in cash, and until this very moment, I had thought cash was god to Bulpitt. I mentioned something of the sort.

"Shelf, you insult me," he said. "I have never, ever put anyone on the road for money alone. That would be....it would be....well, you know." He was still rubbing his thumb and forefinger together, proving to me that first impressions are best. I returned to thinking of Bulpitt as a crass, money-grubbing martinet, which was as it should be.

And yes, I did know what it would be. It would be unethical, and I wasn't at all surprised Bulpitt couldn't locate that word in his limited vocabulary.

Bulpitt continued, for the rest of that week, to ask me at odd moments why I had not confiscated Captain Africa's mobile phone. I muttered something about the sovereignty of the individual, human rights, that sort of thing. I didn't mention the man's biceps, which appeared to me about the same circumference as a Christmas goose.

The one thing Bulpitt never raised was the question of why, of the hundreds of students we've had, Captain Africa was the only one to pay in cash. Even celebrities have their people pay for them from credit accounts kept for such purposes. Even that Provenzano woman paid by cheque. I wondered, at the time, if she had connections to the Sicilian-American crime family. But no. Not possible. This was England, after all. The same nation so cunningly referred to by the Germans as Grosses Britannien. It sounds better in Italian: Gran Bretagne. You have to say it while making hand motions, upward on the Gran, a pause in midair, then a swoop upward, open palm, for the entire Bretagne. I swear. If you don't do that, you can't pronounce it. Especially not if you're British.

Of course, the Provenzano woman—actually, her name was Gina Lolloputtanesca—didn't last long. I have no idea whether she learned to drive or not. What I did know was that I personally could not teach the woman to drive.

"Gina, you need to glance in your rearview mirror, your wing mirror and briefly over your shoulder to be sure no one is overtaking you. Then gently pull forward and out around the car parked ahead."

"No, I can't," she said.

"Why not?"

"Because it is in the way and if I go around it, then I will be on the wrong side of the street."

"Yes, I know. For a few moments. But that's why we look first to make sure we are not going to collide with someone trying to overtake both of us from behind. And why we look ahead to be sure we won't come nose to nose with someone proceding toward us."

"I still can't do it."

"Is it a problem of not knowing how to turn the steering wheel? You just grasp it in one hand, then slide it through that hand with the other hand, gently pressing down on the accelerator. We start on streets with little traffic so you can get the feel for pushing the steering wheel through your hands to the proper turn, and going forward at the same time. Now just start it very slowly. Look first. Then go. I'll help you."

"I can't do it."

"Mrs. Provenzano, if you don't do it, you can't drive. The only alternative is to go backward until you reach a corner, back around it, straighten out and go in another direction. But that defeats the purpose of driving...."

"But...."

"OK. I've checked. It's OK right now. NOW, slowly turn the wheel and gently push on the accelerator."

We went nowhere.

"NOW!"

Nothing.

"Not now. There's a car approaching," I said, keeping the exasperation out of my voice with a supreme effort of will.

"I know."

"After he passes us, then we can go."

"No. I can't."

"Why?"

"I told you."

"That's ridiculous." I began to sweat. "You cannot drive if you will not go around stopped objects. Cars. Buses. Bicycles. Trash bins that roll into the roadway. Dogs sleeping. Sheep for crying out loud on Dartmoor."

"No."

"OK. Let's change places and I'll show you how it's done."

I did.

We changed back.

"I can't do it."

I wanted to say, "You're fucking nuts." She could have had megalophobia. Nah, it doesn't mean the erroneous concept held by George W. Bush that he had the cojones and intelligence to lead the former colonies. That's megalomania. Megalophobia is simply fear of large objects. A car is a large object, ergo....

Or maybe it was simply motorphobia…fear of cars…except that she had managed to get into one. Frankly, I cannot find a Latin name for fear of passing parked cars. If I knew one, I would have told her what her problem was. But all I said was, "Nuts. Let's change seats again and we'll go back to the office. Maybe you can schedule a lesson with another instructor. But Mrs. Provenzano, neither I nor anyone else can teach a person to drive who will not go around stationary objects. Perhaps you should just plan to have Family take you places." I was sure I had said Family with a Capital F, they way the Mafia says words like godfather. She had, after all, arrived for her lesson in a black car with darkened windows that afternoon. It left me wondering whether she had ever told her husband to bring home some cannoli. I bet she did. She was quite a large woman. That heft had to come from something.

For those of you who never saw *The Godfather*, or were too high on pot to pay attention or were an Italian-American from the American South and therefore had no knowledge whatsoever of your culinary ethnic heritage….

Anyway, in an early scene, the wife of one of the wise guys tells him not to forget the cannoli on his way home. He forgets, what with having to whack another wise guy. As I recall, all this took place near one of the New York City bridge toll booths. But the wise guy's friend remembers. About to leave the car with the stiff in it parked at the side of one of the New York city parkways, a desolate stretch not unlike the fens of East Anglia, the wise guy who popped "Paulie" tells his companion, "Leave the gun. Take the cannoli." That's how important cannoli is. Paulie is lying there like a blood-spouting watering can, and Rocco is worried more about his compadre's cannoli than the killing they just completed.

###
**Cannoli also appears in 1990's *The Godfather Part III*.
Connie Corleone kills Don Altobello by feeding him poisoned
cannoli.—Researched by Prof. G. Barker**
###

To prove that I'm up to date, though, Tony Soprano talked about
cannoli a lot. You don't know who Tony Soprano was? Even in
the UK, people know who Tony Soprano is. But I'll be kind and
tell you, in case you've been living rough in the fens or down on
Dartmoor in the remains of a hut circle at 1,000 cold, windswept,
Sky-less feet on an ancient tor: Tony Soprano was a wise-guy on
a long-running US show about Sicilian-Americans called,
quaintly enough, *The Sopranos*. The only singing anyone did,
though, was to the cops about other wise guys in return for
favours. You want some cannoli? Notoriously hard to find, even
in Italian restaurants in the UK. You can make your own, though.
I know it must be easy because my wife does it, frequently, and
as noted earlier, she's not much into cooking. I'll get hold of her
recipe and put it in the back.

All Mrs. Provenzano said before leaving the ranks of learner
drivers—forever, I hope—was, "O.K."

She got out; I drove home. I don't know whether she ever
booked a lesson at Cars From 'L or anywhere else. I don't care. I
hope she never got behind the wheel again, in fact. Life's too
short…and with people like her somehow eventually getting onto
the UK's roads, it might be shorter still.

The Mob aside, it was suggestive, I always thought, that
Bulpitt never mentioned the African's cash again. Knowing
him—and how he had it in for me—I'm surprised he didn't
suggest the payments were bigger than the amounts I had turned
in to the office.

But then, as much as Bulpitt has had it in for me, I'd happily have had it in for him, too, if all that yoga had not filled me with such peace and joy that the best I could do was think, "Screw you," whenever Bulpitt pulled yet another stunt aimed at me.

At the time, with visions of central African thugs swirling in my mind, I reminded Bulpitt that no less than former UK foreign secretary Lord Owen had suggested assassinating Amin. While Lord Owen was roundly criticized over that idea, it doesn't seem that bad in retrospect. I mean, the BBC reported that Amin feasted on the bodies of some of his victims and threw other corpses—of the hundred of thousands he murdered—to the crocodiles. I'm not saying my student would have done anything remotely like this; I'm just saying perhaps there should be some sort of background check on people who are alone with instructors in a moving vehicle on all sorts of roads from city streets to lonely rural lanes because of the harm they might do, irrespective of the odd crushed wheelie bin and so on.

FIVE

Diamonds on the Soles of Her Shoes

It's odd how, when you've got time to kill and don't know how much time, bits of songs will go through your head. I admit to having silently sung *The Ant's Picnic* (you know, "the ants go marching two by two, hurrah, hurrah") while waiting for interminable meditation hours to end during my yoga instructor days. This time, Paul Simon's *Graceland* album seemed to be top of mind. "Diamonds on the soles of her shoes," was a frequent number, playing in the mists of my sleep-deprived mind. But "Fifty Ways to Leave Your Lover" also made frequent runs. I wondered if I was getting ready to leave wife number 11, the American who made good sausage and Italian tatas…I mean tatties…despite her inability to do more than book a table at a restaurant at dinner time. Unless you wanted to mangia on some great Italian food. Her sausage and tatties wasn't bangers and mash; it was luganica and a tasty potato-tomato concoction. But good British ros' bif (as the French would say) and spuds from my wife? Not bloody likely.

If one is sitting in a freezing cold room with nothing to look at except a locked door, a scratched wooden table, a plastic chair and the big one-way mirror through which you just know they are looking at you, you've got to occupy your mind, or you will go nuts. Prisoners in Vietnam, I have read, often reconstructed entire books of the Bible when they were kept in solitary. Tiger cages, I think those prison cells were called. They weren't cold; they were warm. Very warm. Broiling. Maybe heat turns one's head to religion. Cold? Cold just puts your mind in suspended animation. Sort of. You know you're cold, and in this case that there was nothing to be done about it. But it also wouldn't last as long as a tiger cage in Vietnam. So the obvious choice was to dwell on happier things, one of which is Paul Simon's *Graceland* album. I went through all of it. I kept hopping off the track, though, into *The Lion Sleeps Tonight*, that old early '60s song with all the whimaways.

Then I got hung up on *You Can Call Me Al* for a couple of hours.

> "Why am I soft in the middle?
> "The rest of my life is so hard!
> "I need a photo-opportunity,
> "I want a shot at redemption!"

Maybe I was getting religion after all. Why else sing silent lyrics about redemption?

Nah. I got hung up on the line "Get these mutts away from me," too.

At last, one of the mutts came in, bearing goodies. Coffee, hot coffee. And the news that my fingerprints were not on the envelopes.

But I'm losing my place.

In fact, I exaggerated earlier about eleven wives. I've read that eleven is a funny number, so I use it a lot. I like to entertain people whom I would otherwise bore to tears. I've only had four wives, including this one, as you might have noticed from an earlier comment. But four is not a funny number.

Perhaps you can forgive me my asides, though, and my claims of excessive use of the registry office ; I'm telling you this amazing tale from memory alone. No notes. No photos. In any case, who would have time for eleven wives? Hollywood types, I suppose, since they do nothing but lie around in the sun most of the year, except for the three weeks they pose in front of cameras and people with actual brain matter under their hair tell them what to say, how to say it, when to say it, where to say it, to whom to say it, how to gesture when they say it, what emotion they should attempt to spread across their visage as they say it….

Right. The least creative people in the theatre are the actors, in my opinion. Mannequins with thick hair, thin tummies and an even thinner excuse for raking in all that loot. I mean, is a couple hours' worth of work—play?—worth $5 million? OK. So it takes a couple of months to shoot that couple of hours. But they don't even have to learn a book full of lines like stage actors. They can learn them about four sentences at a time, as films are shot in small segments. Even a parrot can do that much.

"Mr. Barker," the donor of cophouse goodies began. "We just have a few questions regarding your involvement with the car in which the body or bodies was found."

"You don't know if it's one or two?"

"Decomposition was well advanced. We are sure there were two carbon-based lifeforms…."

I began to laugh. Carbon-based lifeforms. Cops that sounded like actors in *Star Trek, the Movie.* Then I noticed his scowl; I didn't need any more cop scowls. So I punted. "I get a lot of those in my line of work," I said.

He looked a question at me. "My students," I said. "Carbon-based lifeforms."

"Oh," he said. "Well, then, the larger one, which was less decomposed, appeared to be a woman. But the smaller one…it could be a large-ish woman, a small man, a very large dog, a juvenile chimpanzee. It will be a while until we have particulars for either one, but particularly that one. However, we need some background information regarding your involvement."

One what? Man or chimp? Woman or large dog? Surely a dog would exhibit (cop speak) a lot more hair than a woman…well, than most women.

And I wished he would stop using the word involvement. I wasn't involved. I knew nothing about it, and that's precisely what I wanted to know. Nothing. But wait. The bigger bag definitely contained a woman? That more or less bagged it for me; it had to be Mrs. B. She made any of my wife's larger-than-life aunts look like Herve Villechaize. Who? The French diminutive actor, or to be politically correct, a little person. WTF? It turns out Villechaize eschewed that PC term and preferred to be called a midget. Suits me. I was awaked from my musings about dwarfism by the dulcet tones of one of my beloved city's finest.

"For example, we understand Mr. Bulpitt's wife is missing. Is that true?"

"I don't know if she's missing. He mentioned that she had been gone for a while. Maybe she has a habit of leaving from time to time. I really wouldn't know. The Bulpitts were not close friends."

"Did you feel any animus toward Mrs. Bulpitt? Or was there some secret involvement that led to that letter addressed to you found beneath the bags?"

Involvement again. "No, no animus, no particular friendship, certainly no "special" friendship. Bulpitt is my boss; Mrs. Bulpitt is my boss's wife, and that's as deep and as wide as our 'involvement' extends."

"What about Mr. Ignatowski?"

"He's on holiday in Poland."

"Are you sure?"

"Of course I'm not SURE sure. He said that's where he was going about a week ago....or at least, I think he did. It could have been more recently...I'm not his best mate, either."

"He has been gone more than a month. Why are you lying about Mr. Ignatowski?"

"I'm not lying. It seemed more recent to me. But we are only colleagues at a driving school. We don't knock back pints together. And it's not like we sit next to each other in an office five days a week. Sometimes our paths cross when we go into the building between students to get some coffee or, if you must know, to take a piss."

He actually pursed his lips. I'd have bet I could make him squirm a lot with my usual gutter mouth. I should have said, "When I go into to squeeze the lemonade out of my wanger." If I had known cops came in the Prude flavour, I would have. Just for fun.

"Let's leave Mr. Ignatowski for a moment. Was that learner car your specific domain? Did others use it?"

"Lots of others used it. Everyone used it from time to time. I admit, I did have a couple of students who were very fond of it, so I would use it for them even when my regular car was not in for servicing, as long as no one else needed it."

"Did other instructors do that?"

"Not that I'm aware of. Why?"

"Let's move on. Which of your students liked that car?"

"Captain Africa, for one."

He raised his eyebrows in a question.

"He was from Central Africa someplace, a real weird guy who spent most of each lesson on his mobile phone...."

"I assume you pulled off the road?????????????"

"No, I just reached over and grabbed the wheel while he talked."

The cop's eyebrows went up. This could be fun.

"No." Freaking flatfoot. Of course we had pulled off the road. We were in ENGLAND, not the United States. You'll get a huge fine if you're caught here yakking and driving. In the U.S., I have been told, it is expected that overscheduled mummies will chat on their mobile while drinking coffee, eating a fast-food all-in-one breakfast, changing the CD, putting on eye makeup and tights, and going 75 mph.

###

Making or taking phone calls when driving will distract you. Research shows that if you're using any mobile phone when driving, you're four times more likely to crash. You also have significantly worse reaction times than someone driving after drinking alcohol at the legal limit.—Directgov website

###

"Mr. Barker, we have homes to go to as well, and I'm sure you're eager to help us...."

"Yes, I am. Sorry. Had I known what you want. But I'll just shut up and you ask the questions."

He "tsked" a couple of times.

"Do you recall the name of this man?"

As if I could ever forget it. Although, he was nowhere near as weird as Manuel. But that's another story. Let's just say Manuel's spandex pants made my macho side emerge to the point that even I wanted to slap me for being a male chauvinist pig.

And on and on it went, back and forth through these questions, for an hour. And then he asked about The Cobra. He didn't call her that, of course. He called her Chloe Barker. Why she had chosen to retain my name is a mystery beyond my ability to solve. I can barely find a missing sock in my own house, so it's not like bearing my moniker would enhance her business profile at all.

I was stunned. Oh, OK. She *is* a private detective. Maybe they all knew each other; how should I know? What did he want to know? Everything, except how many times a week we had made love back when we were married to each other.

"Hardly ever," I said, and his eyebrows went up. I was answering a question he hadn't asked. But he obviously figured out what I was answering about, and smirked.

He was obviously questioning my manhood, by now, if not my sanity. The Cobra is a lovely woman. She's tall and thin, but there is something sensuous and sinuous about her carriage—and for a slender woman, she has a nice caboose as well. I can imagine he thought I was either gay or nuts, or alternatively, a sexual predator. Actually, I had just been too relaxed. If I had done that yoga thing much longer, I think I could easily have been embalmed and buried before anyone figured out that my ability to remain perfectly still and almost breathless for long periods was, actually, a form of life. It was odd, really, how relaxed I was during this experience. Or maybe I was just brain dead after those hours of silently singing, "This is the story of how we begin to remember; This is the powerful pulsing of love in the vein…." from the "Under African Skies" cut of *Graceland*.

So I told him about the yoga and got the distinct impression the was taking frequent apparent sips from his cold coffee to hide more smirking.

"Just a few more questions," he finally said. "What do you know about diamonds? Do you buy jewellery for your wife?"

I answered. "Nothing and hardly ever."

"Hardly ever? Did you memorize that phrase, or what? What does it mean? Once a year, more, less…what?"

"OK. Since the engagement and wedding rings, nothing. Not one piece. So I'm a cheapskate. But she's the one with all the money; she buys what she wants. Me? I buy her any kind of flowers from Tesco she wants, as long as they are in the 'Quick Sale' display. OK?"

He was finished then, and told me I could go. What he wanted to know about my jewellery purchases for I had no idea. And what was all that about Iggy? Was he missing? Poor guy. I wonder if he decided to stay in Poland with his old mother he went to see so often. He had no family in the UK, and it had to be hard for her with only son to be living away from home, even though he was over 50. She had to be ancient. Well, at least 70.

But The Cobra. Why did they bring her into it? I had been trying not to think about her, to think it was too bad we had split, since I could apparently use her help about now. The cops hadn't cautioned me. Just a little chat, they said. But I watched TV. I knew what that usually meant. Nothing good. Not for the person they were chatting with. But I hadn't DONE it. Hadn't done what? To whom? It was early days yet, and I was scared my personal fright theatre might have a longer life span than my delicate sensibilities could tolerate.

***

While the interview with the cops had been mercifully brief when it finally happened, getting sprung took longer. It's a good thing the UK has virtually outlawed gun ownership, because I can imagine people inventing miniature weaponry, small enough to be hidden under a good hairpiece, for the express purpose of dealing with the intellectually challenged non-enforcement personnel one finds in any police station. Well, at least in the one in my city, a fen-ringed metropolis of many lovely old buildings, a magnificent cathedral for those who go in for that sort of thing, and the usual UK platoon of Eurostyle wannabe homely high-rise monstrosities with Scandinavian primary color blocks of tin or something interspersed with non-opening expanses of glass.

So why, you might ask, did I not get home for two nights? I was sprung within hours, all warmed up inside by the fine machine-dispensed coffee they gave me by way of apology, I guess.

When I finally was able to leave the police station—after they finally located the clerk who had stashed for safekeeping my wallet, mobile phone, Swiss Army knife, Italian phrasebook, three packets of Starbucks Viva (to cope with the birdbath water Bulpitt provides as coffee at the office since he just doesn't think staff and students are worth spending real coffee money on), and my Kindle—it was only 3 a.m. I knew my wife wouldn't be worried; the cops had called her to tell her where I was.

OK. She probably was worried simply because she did know where I was. But I was even more worried. Not about where I was, but about *where I was*. I mean, how does someone who was once a respected university lecturer become embroiled in a murder at least tangentially connected to his place of employment? I was having what many call a dark night of the soul. See? There was a reason for those Paul Simon lyrics.

After a decent cop took me back to what I hoped was still my place of employment, I drove my regular learner car to a secluded place I knew, surrounded by misty fens, and spent the night pondering my condition.

By sun-up, only a couple of hours later in a British summer, even one as cold as this one, I was no more enlightened than I had been during those years when I enlightened others in the yoga studio. Actually, I was more confused than I'd ever been.

Still, I'm not a total yobbo, so I called home at a decent hour—six a.m.—and told my wife I would be home the next morning, that I had to be alone to think.

You don't think 6 a.m. is a decent hour? Then you're not married to an American with a Puritan work ethic who demands getting up with the birds so you can work. In her case, working is spelled s-h-o-p-p-i-n-g. And yes, we do live beyond our means. Or we would, except for her divorce settlement. Fortunately, her ex-husband was so rotten that she was awarded about half of his multi-million-dollar investment portfolio flat out, plus alimony, even if she remarried. Or at least, that's the story she told me when we met, and I had no reason to question it. Not even after I met all the relatives with the bulges under their jackets, the bent noses and the funny nicknames—Louie the Loudmouth, Stanley "Syracuse" Sosagruba....

So why do I work at all?

What else would I do? I don't have a single hobby. Not one. I don't fish. I don't play games on greensward. I don't cut coupons, either for the Co-op or the kind that rich people cut when investing, whatever the heck that means.

I once began collecting shot glasses from every city I visited, but they just languished in a drawer. I used two at a time, not because I thought the only way to get a double was to use two separate shot glasses. No, it was because my wife claimed she could actually taste it if I poured her Hendrick's gin into and out of the same shot glass I had used to put the Plymouth in my G&T. Sure, I could have simply reversed the order of pour; I'm sure I wouldn't care even if I could tell. But at least this gave me an excuse to use two of my 432 (not really...about 40) shot glasses. Yes, I do exaggerate. It is the hallmark, I believe, of an empty life.

"You could rotate them," wife number three had once said to me. All my wives drink gin, although I certainly don't question them about their spirits preferences before dating them. Why they all drink gin is a mystery, especially since two of the four are not Brits, Brits having an affinity for gin equal to the completely unwarranted affinity already hyper Arabs have for drinking strong coffee loaded with sugar. Indeed, I have long thought that the way to defuse the apparent anger of the Arab world toward the west would be to embargo coffee and sugar shipments to the south and east of the Mediterranean. But every time I mention it, I get whacked verbally—if not physically—by someone who thinks I'm a horrible bigot. But if we could cut down their caffeine and sugar highs, it might work. Since they are forbidden by their religion to drink booze and they aren't far enough east to embrace Zen, what other choice do we have? I'd suggest it to the politicians, but I don't believe I'd like to be identified as a nutjob by the investigative arm of Her Majesty's Secret Service, for instance. So I keep my yap shut. But I still think it's a great idea.

Anyway, I told wife number three that then I'd have to open the drawer the shot glasses were in and make choices. Not one choice, but two. And what if I ended up choosing one from a holiday she knew I'd been on with wife number one or number two? Would she get all wobbly then and threaten to cry? Nope. Not worth it. And truth to tell, there are some places I've been that being reminded of would make me cry. Real men don't cry. So....

The thing is, though, I'm more likely to cry about the places I loved and probably won't see again than about the really painful ones. Like Aruba. What a bitch that trip was. Mainly because wife number….ummm…..number….well, one of them was acting like a cross between Molly Goldberg and Angelina Jolie…before her weird papa straightened her out. Jon Voight was never my favorite actor, but after he began to support that imbecile George W. Bush…well, Americans have strange ways. I'll say no more. Except that Angelina is not my favorite actress, either, because even after Jon-boy straightened her out, she still thinks the sun rises for her alone and she alone can dismiss it for the night. Can't imagine what she was like before. Anyway, that's what wife number…right, it WAS number two…was acting like on that holiday.

But who, you might ask, was Molly Goldberg?

"Who is Molly Goldberg?" I had asked wife number two, opening the mail and finding a cookbook from the States falling out.

"You don't know Molly Goldberg?" she said, incredulous.

Yes, well, we Brits are just deprived. "No."

"Actually, it's the stage name of an actress, Gertrude Berg, who played a character called Molly Goldberg on TV in the early 1950s."

"So? What's a cookbook got to do with it?" I asked. I wanted to add, and what are you buying a cookbook for. But sometimes discretion is the better part of wimpiness.

"Look, Bubela [all my wives have brought one or more ethnic idioms to the party, which is how I expanded my academic vocabulary into one more useful for telling tales about others, or even myself]…"Look, Bubela, the show was a sort of Jewish-American *East Enders*. Molly Goldberg was a prototypical Jewish mother, making chicken soup…"

"Jewish penicillin," I contributed, winning a big smile from wife number two. I was learning.

"Making chicken soup and meddling in the lives of her friends and families, but usually for a good cause," wife number two had said. "I like bagels, and I can't find traditional good ones here—just those things with chocolate bits in them or other goofy flavors—so I'm going to make them."

If you're thinking wife number two was American as well a wife number four, you'd be correct. I figure we are all basically one tribe anyway. I don't mean the whole world or anything quite as New Age as that. I mean Brits and Yanks. You might have noticed I still refer to that landmass as the former colonies. So I figured I would give equal time to those colonies in terms of the marital bed and my scintillating company.

Wife number one was a Brit; number two was a Yank; number three—the lovely Cobra—was a Brit. Number four is a Yank. If I find I'm on the loose again and need to get married once more, I guess I'll have to make it twice to make the numbers work out. Fortunately, my marriages never last long, so there's still time.

I looked at the recipe in the Goldberg Jewish Foods Bible According to My Wife Number Two…whatever her name was. (Look, if I bothered with her name, I'd have to bother with her attributes. And if I did that, who knew? I might get hung up again as I seemed to be doing with The Cobra. Couldn't afford it. Wife number two will suffice as ID.)

The bagel recipe required making bread, that is, letting yeast dough rise a couple of times. Then you were supposed to pull it apart into smaller lumps and form them into circles. It also required dunking the dough circles into a big pot of boiling water before baking them. This was to make the bagels soft inside and chewy outside. I never actually participated, but I was obliged to watch a number of times because if I didn't, and failed to drink in the priceless information that bagels were chewy on the outside and soft on the inside because of the dunking, my wife would quiz me about it. Really. She had a jones for bagel knowledge, to use an American term.

"My cousin lost her first baby tooth in a bagel," wife number two told me the first time she sat me down on the kitchen stool to watch the magic. "That's how chewy they are, the real ones. I'm sure they could pull off crowns, maybe even pull out fillings. Have you been to the dentist lately?"

I hadn't. But I wasn't worried. Wife number two was as unlikely to actually make those bagels again, I thought (erroneously, as it turned out) as she was to make me a full English breakfast, including the black pudding, grilled tomato, mushrooms and baked beans. I have yet to find a wife who will consistently do that. Actually, I have yet to find one who will make me much of a breakfast at all. The two Brits have no excuse. I understand Americans eat things on the run—yoghurt bars and Sugar Cane Plantation Double Soy-Milk Lattes with a drizzle of faux-caramel made from discarded sticky notes on top. Maybe I've found the key.

Maybe I should just affirm that whatever woman will cook a Full English Breakfast will get the job. My ex-wives, who wouldn't, ended up getting job seekers' allowance checks after the job was over—that is, we divorced, and they were collecting alimony checks. In short, they were all on the dole. The Shelf Barker Memorial Dole, if you will. And don't tell me I can't use the word memorial since I am still alive. I lost a little bit of myself with each of those failures, but Semi-Memorial Dole wouldn't sound right.

###

A Full English breakfast is very like a Full Irish, Full Scottish, Full Welsh, or in any region, simply called a fry-up, since almost everything is fried, sometimes including the toast. The breakfast must have an egg and sausage and/or bacon and toast or fried bread. It should also have one or more of the following: black or white pudding, sauteed mushrooms, grilled tomato, grilled kippers, baked beans. Washed down with large mug of tea. These days, things once fried are often grilled, but it's still a fry-up.—Researched by Prof. G. Barker

###

If I decide to make breakfast preparation a prerequisite for marriage to me, my current wife won't get the job, either. "Ick," she said when I first described my preferred morning repast. "I'll make you a couple of scrambled eggs or even fried eggs. I might make you a poached egg on toast. But that black pudding stuff? No. No way. Not in my house. It stinks. It's ugly. It's blood for crying out loud. Why don't you just cut yourself and bleed onto your plate instead?"

"I'm not a pig," I replied.

Sometimes raised eyebrows convey quite a bit.

I love attitude in a woman. Fortunately, I've been amply sated on that score, by any number of wives. Four, actually, as abashedly admitted.

***

I was gone for two days...or more like a day and a half, and I wasn't alone the whole time. I admit it. I phoned a former wife, the aforementioned third wife, The Cobra. I drove to London to see her. We spent all day talking. I swear. Topped it off with a drunken evening and we both sacked out. Alone. She in her bed, I on the sofa. Cross my heart.

Why would I go see my third wife? Simple. She was the love of my life, and she was also a private investigator. And the cops had asked me about her. Why? How did they even know I knew her? I mean, had they done a background check on me? And if so, why? I was getting a little paranoid, although not quite to the point of wearing an aluminium hat.

And why had I divorced her? In fact, she divorced me. It was during the yoga years, and she just couldn't take my peaceable countenance after she had spent the day chasing absconding parents and the night huddled in a car hoping for a photo of a cheating spouse. I'll grant you that we met at the ashram where I worked. She had arrived there as a student, hoping to find ways to chill after 12 hours of chasing errant fathers (or deadbeat dads, as the Yanks call them) that didn't involve alcohol or someone else's husband. OK. So she succeeded on the first; she drinks very little now, mainly chanting *Om mani padme hom* when she's over-stressed. As for other people's husbands…well, I was married to number two when The Cobra and I crossed paths, a platitude that soon turned into locked horns. However you want to take that.

Did I mention I exaggerated about eleven wives? Oh, right. I did. Four is the accurate number.

When I was married to Chloe (sounds good with Cobra), I felt like a chump. There I was, togged out in yoga pants and logo shirt, pasting a goofy grin on my face, instructing flabby middle-aged women in The Downward Facing Dog or One-Legged Pigeon or leading them in the Sun Salute, all the while breathily encouraging them to think of themselves as divine creations of the Prime Spirit.

Before you ask, there are two reasons to give instructions in a soft, breathy way. First, one is not supposed to interrupt their reverie, or whatever they are going into via your ministrations.

Second, you know that erroneous belief people have that all male ballet dancers are gay? They also have that concept about male yoga instructors. While I may not be the most macho of men, neither am I gay...although I am not a gay-basher.

"What? How can that be, Shelf?" you might ask, considering my myriad other non-politically correct beliefs. It's simple. I don't bash people for their god-given endowments, which include sex, sexual preference, age, intelligence. Well, except for Bulpitt on that last. I figure cultural stuff is fair game, though, because you can change it if you want. It's an elective, unlike your skin color, for example. My wife, for instance, is Italian, but she's not a mob doll.

So, anyway, there I was, day in and day out, virtually whispering, "Deep breath, deep breath."

Stentorian breathing sounds returned to me from the jiggly flesh overspilling about half the yoga pants in the room.

"Like this," I would instruct, gently pushing their swollen ankles into position atop their pudgy knees.

Why did I do it? Simple. I had actually been frozen out of the university job, not because of the laboratory incident, but because I was not politically correct. I had the audacity to suggest, more than once, that students think for themselves and also that Darwinism had something to recommend it. You will note that my political correctness errors did not involve those innate attributes I mentioned above, but rather the students' unfortunate enculturation into the Society of Fundamentalist Bellybutton Contemplators.

And no, I didn't teach at Cambridge or Oxford. Obviously. I taught at a little-known UK outpost of a US Bible college. I kindly refer to now it as Snakehandler U., but it's real name was The University of God Almighty and Little Fishes. OK. That's not it either. I won't give its real name because, to tell the truth, I'm afraid of them. Their administrative staff. Anyone who ever had anything to do with them—from laid-off kitchen staff to professors who espouse the subversive practice of rational thought—is afraid of them. Few people know this, but there is a religious mafia, and unbelievers are dealt with severely.

Let me give you an example of a conversation I had with another professor.

"Damn it," I said, "That cute but unaccountably ignorant red-dot has done it again, bought her paper from some scum company that charges students with more money than brains to write the thing." I'm not prejudiced: I expect Indian students to be bright, and it sucker punches me when they are not. That's my excuse for the slur, and I'm sticking to it.

"Language," hissed a female teacher—few of those on board, I can tell you, since it's hard to get any who are dedicated to the cause who aren't barefoot and pregnant. Barefoot, in an English winter session, is no picnic. I can't comment on the pregnant part.

As I said, I tend to use politically incorrect language quite often. Frankly, some people are so ridiculously oversensitive that I do it on purpose, when I know they are the type to raise bogus objections, to wind them up. Why bogus objections? Mainly because most of them are simply spouting something the thought police told them to do; they have no more concern for the feeling of red dots, towelheads, frogs or wogs than a lamp post.

As for me, I quite like being referred to as a ros biff by the frogs. My wife even calls me ros biff. After all, Brits DO eat roast beef to excess, so how can it be pejorative if it fits? Sometimes my wife calls me a limey. I find both so-called insults endearing. I wish I could find a pet name for her, but I'm afraid whatever I came up with might sound offensive to her extended family in America, and I'm still in favour of the idea that he was boiled in oil—or dumped in a vat of chemicals in fact—for where Jimmy Hoffa ended up. I know, it's only their culture I'd be lampooning, right? So no problem, according to my own standards of political correctness? Did I mention this is the Mafia I'm talking about? The same Mafia that offed Jimmy Hoffa.

Who's Jimmy Hoffa? Long-time president of the International Brotherhood of Teamsters, an American union, who disappeared in 1975. His body was never found, and he was declared dead in 1982. I always thought he was Italian.

"I thought all Italian last names ended in a vowel," I said to my wife one night when I was musing on the state of humanity when she told me her clan—the Italians—didn't own Hoffa.

"Not all Italian names end in a vowel. For instance, there's Tschurtschenthaler."

I just stood there, waiting for her to explain herself.

"Tschurtschenthaler. It's in the Italian phone directory. Look it up."

"First of all, we don't own an Italian phone directory. Second, it's obviously a German name. Germans do live in Italy; a lot of them live in Alto-Adige," I reminded her. "Just because a name is in the Italian phone directory doesn't mean it's an Italian name. For all we know, there might be a bunch of Smiths in there."

She deflected, of course. "Anyway, Hoffa wasn't Italian."

I snorted.

"No, really, he was of Dutch extraction." I always liked the way Americans used "extraction" to explain their ethnic heritage. As if they were a bad tooth that had to come out. What about other words one could use? For example, what about lineage? So I asked her.

"Too highfalutin," she said. Another Americanism. I looked up "falutin." I didn't expect to find it, but there it was. "…expressed in or marked by the use of high-flown bombastic language: pompous." OK. So what's wrong with pompous? Or maybe, I suggested, grandiloquent. She rolled her eyes, stretched like our cat, Mr. Bumpy, and slithered off the sofa in search of sustenance. That is, she went to the larder to extract a nibble, a nosh, a snack, a small nutritional addition to her daily intake of comestibles.

I said most of that stuff to her, and she just lifted a finger in my direction. Only one. She does it the American way. She told me once it takes too much energy to raise two fingers, and besides, it might look to some either like a peace sign or Richard Nixon giving his version of a thumbs up. Biff followed her, ever mindful that she was, underneath it all, a dog person and some toothsome titbit was likely to be tossed his way.

I replied with one of my favourite quotes from one of my favourite movies, *Coming to America*, the Eddie Murphy film I mentioned earlier. I cooed into my wife's ear, "There is a very fine line between love and nausea." It was said by King Jaffe Joffer, played by James Earl Jones. I tried for the timbre of his voice, but I think I failed. I might be tall enough, but I'm not big enough. My wife did her cute barfing noises. She actually sounds a lot like Mr. Bumpy when he offers us some ABC food in the morning after wolfing down his first tribute of tuna, one of many throughout the day.

None of this discussion of cats and films and names and all things Italian means anything. Except when the New Jersey and/or Brooklyn relatives are visiting, we have a very good marriage. I am reasonably expectant that it might last. She's a good cook, when she cooks, and only Italian. I'm a good…well, she's an Italian girl. What to you think?

Eater. I meant eater.

***

But back to the conversation on campus. After my unfortunate lapse into the politically incorrect language of the gutter, one of my many adversaries among the faculty took me to task. "You know, it's not right in God's world to make fun of his other creatures," he said, his Jim Bakker-hair bobbing atop his amazingly low forehead.

He was jabbing a finger at me, making a point. I fully expected wild swooping of arms, like James Brown, godfather of soul, moon walking across the stage in *The Blues Brothers*. Without the crimson robe, though, it wouldn't be nearly as effective, but possibly twice as funny. This was not vibrant black guy; this guy was a short, scrawny, simian pie-faced fool (I got that "fool" stuff from Mr. T, one of my heroes) in an ill-fitting Burberry's knock-off suit and a badly knotted tie slumped down well below his only just noticeable Adams apple. His voice matched.

I raised my eyebrows, which just sort of happened every time this fool's tiny voice came squirting out of his lipless mouth.

"Creatures? They aren't creatures," I informed him. "They're people."

Now he was beginning to get nervous. I could tell because his tiny rib cage was compressing further and his legs had drawn up enough that only his toes reached the floor. But to be fair, it was a relatively high sofa. They had recently redone the faculty lounge in Early Inquisition so there wasn't a deep, comfy place to sit between there and my former shrink's office.

"Don't pretend you've misunderstood my meaning, Barker." (Ooh, tough guy.) "You know perfectly well what I meant. You have the worst habit of demeaning others by the way you speak about them…."

"Oh, surely not the worst," I stepped on his line. "Didn't ol' JC call some of his compatriots thieves and so on?"

Spluttering commenced.

"But he hung around with them just the same, didn't he?" I asked. "Even if he thought they might have been Samaritans or something. Or maybe demons. Right. He hung out in the desert with a demon, as I recall. Are you trying to tell me that I have to be better than the Son of God to be acceptable to you? Are you trying to tell me I have to be better than a *tax collector*? One of the disciples was a tax collector." I fairly screamed the last part.

"You're confusing apples and oranges," my simian friend announced. "Jesus said 'Render unto Caesar…'."

"That which is Caesar's and unto God that which is God's. Yes, I know," I said, calmly, slowly, ever the peacemaker, I. "But how the effing hell could they tell one quid from another? Were some marked Caesar and others marked God? Hey, they wouldn't be marked God anyway. I think the feckers called the dude Yahweh, didn't they?"

Fraulein Doktor Mengele hissed "Language" again. Sorry, I meant to write Magdalen, after the putative wife of Christ, a position I often thought the good Fraulein Doktor thought she herself warranted. She was, after all, a virgin…and if there was a god, would so remain until judgment day.

Professor Simian jumped down. I jumped up. You wouldn't have had to measure to tell I was a full head taller, and at least that much more amused. I had deflected his chance to launch into a full-blown sermon about being kind to our fellow man, or woman, even when said man or woman was nowhere nearby.

I really think I preferred making my wife slither off the sofa to making Professor Monkey-face scamper out of a room. He was just funny. My wife, on the other hand, was actually fairly alluring when she took umbrage and expressed her distaste for whatever I had done NOW with her body language. She got a lovely look of disdain on that perfectly sculpted face. Her full lips curled into a derisive snarl. She pulled her shoulders back, which set off her ample endowment, and when she got up, she tightened her glutes just enough to render all imagination about what was under her skin-tight jeans useless. Ah, lovely. No wonder I liked pissing her off so much.

By the way, just because I said my wife slithered off the couch, don't think I get her confused with THE Cobra. Impossible. THE Cobra is thin to the point of scrawny. Mean to the point of Thatcher. Smart to the point of Einstein. My wife? Not that thin. Not fat. Just curvy. Not mean except when I deserve it, although knowing her ethnic heritage (extraction?), I don't push my luck. And she's smart enough. Just enough. Not too much. My male ego couldn't take too much. Maybe that was part of the split with The Cobra.

But now, here I was with The Cobra, peaceably talking over the dilemma that had so recently presented itself, and wondering how I had never noticed how beautiful her perfectly sculpted, Anglo-Saxon face was, with its lovely complexion, "natural" blonde hair, and wide blue eyes. After dismissing virtually everything about her and her life way back when because it was too messy and brought with it the potential for mayhem against her person, or even mine, I was embroiled in something that was her stock in trade. I needed her help, and she was willing to give it. Perhaps I should call her Chloe. I did call her Chloe to her face, when she opened the door that Saturday morning.

"Chloe?" she said. "I thought you usually called me The Cobra."

Caught. I just stood there opening and closing my mouth until she finally laughed and invited me in.

"Plus, you stink."

I did. She pointed me toward the shower. She found an old jogging suit of her own that stretched to fit me, sort of, and tossed my clothes, socks to shirt, into the washer. I felt a little bit like Cary Grant in the film *Bringing Up Baby* when Katharine Hepburn takes his clothes and he ends up in her frilly negligee. I was hoping I wouldn't have to chase a small dog over a large yard looking for an historic bone, as Grant did. But with The Cobra, who knew?

As it turned out, I spilled my guts.

SIX

The Look of Love

I realize that, in using Brooklynese from 1940s crime films, I risk sounding like James Cagney in *Angels with Dirty Faces*, or maybe Edward G. Robinson in anything he ever appeared in.

I figure it's better than sounding like what I was. Scared. Frightened. Terrified.

The Co....I mean Chloe settled me down with some breakfast. A lot of breakfast, *almost* a Full English, actually. Except for the toadstools. I hate toadstools. I wouldn't tell my wife that. I wouldn't want to spoil her belief that by not cooking me a Full English, she was totally depriving me. You can't be deprived of mushrooms. Who wants to eat a fungus? I can't even call them mushrooms. They aren't good enough for that. Toadstools is good enough for them. And then, over a second cup of coffee, looking out over Battersea Park, I spilled my guts.

It was worth it. The Cobra lived in York Mansions, a venerable block of flats built when life was a lot less complex than now. When people had servants who cooked their masters' food on coal stoves. The Cobra's corner flat offered great views from the kitchen sink, both the Albert Bridge and the Battersea Bridge. I had loved that area since I was a small boy, when my grandfather told me that during WWII, if troops were marched across the Albert Bridge, they had to break step or risk the bridge falling in. Very reassuring, but to a young boy, the stuff smash-'em-up dreams are made of.

Before I began telling The C....Chloe what had happened, I engineered a trip to the sink to wash my hands, took some time over it as if I were planning my remarks, but mainly, I just needed a touchstone, a sense of place and past and me in what had been a very, very odd 48 hours. Even for me.

I sat down at length...not a single exasperated sigh from my ex-wife while she waited, which might have meant she was daydreaming about anything but me, or that she had mellowed, or that she figured whatever it was I had gotten into was so far beyond redemption....

Anyway, I began.

"They didn't caution me," I said. She nodded.

"They asked me questions about Bulpitt (she rolled her eyes) and Mrs. Bulpitt and Ignatz."

"Who's Ignatz?"

"A Polish guy. He's a good teacher. But he goes AWOL every so often to see his old widowed mother in Poland. I thought he was gone for a week this time. The cop said it was more like a month."

"Observant."

(Shut up.)

"They asked if I ever bought my wife jewellery."

"I hope you said no. They don't like liars. Unless you've reformed?"

"Cute."

"They asked me about the letter with my name on it under the bags, sort of. They asked me about the necklace. I don't really know if they have confirmed that the one apparently containing Mrs. Bulpitt's necklace also contained Mrs. Bulpitt. Until I saw that piece of bling, I'd have been sure Bulpitt never gave her any bespoke jewellery, that there might be thousands just like it.

Maybe it was junk jewellery, but it sure looked real to me. And Bulpitt was more in a tizzy about that than he was about the dripping bag possibly containing his missing wife. I can't imagine them being able to confirm her identity that quickly. Those bodies were....I can't even imagine. They were dripping! What could be left to identify from a pool of organic matter with fluid-drenched fabric on it?"

I was wheezing. For me, that was a long speech, but I couldn't shut up.

"What did the cops say to you?" Chloe asked.

"Nothing. Well, not much of anything. Unaccountably, they asked if I had ever been to Poland. Odd question."

"Well?"

"Chloe! Of course not. Why would I go to Poland? I don't even like kielbasa. I'm not Catholic. I don't need to see where the late Karol Wojtyla came from. And England is cold enough."

"Who's Carol?"

"Who was Karol. And it's not a she. Karol Wojtyla was better known as Pope John Paul II."

"And I would know that how?"

Chloe was an oddity in England, a member of the Society of Friends, otherwise known as Quakers. I had no idea, to this day, what they believed. But I know they didn't like crooks much, despite former, disgraced and now deceased U.S. President Richard "I am not a crook" Nixon having been one, US variety. Maybe Chloe was correcting the damage Nixon wrought on the Quaker image. Not that her main line of business was catching crooks; it was catching marital cheaters and people who skipped out on landlords and suchlike. Sometimes she just had to make reports on people because other people wanted to know more about them. Was that legal? I mean, could you just snoop on people? Apparently, as long as all the information was readily available in public documents or by asking neighbours and friends, and you didn't want to use the information for evil deeds. I guess my mind wandered, but Chloe snapped me back.

"Off on the planet Karma again, Shelf?" she asked. "You had that dreamy look about you that I once loved...."

Did she sound wistful. Nah. I could see by that shy smile and the downcast eyes that she was winding me up. So I returned to Now.

"They also asked if I had ever been to Italy. I told them no to that, too. Two odd questions, I thought."

"Hmmm....."

"I sort of wonder if they have hauled in Miracle, too. She's Italian this week."

Chloe rolled her eyes. "Not even cops could be that stupid. But who else did they question?"

Frankly, I didn't know who else they had questioned. Possibly everyone who had a key to that spare car. Which would have meant Miracle. In fact, she kept the keys to the cabinet that had spare keys to all the cars.

"Shelf," Chloe said before long. "You don't know who the body is, or bodies if the other one *is* a body. You don't know how they died. You don't know who the police have questioned. It seems to me, you don't know anything. Therefore, why worry?"

It was true that I didn't know anything, and not just about this situation, either, as she and all the other wives had been at pains to assure me from the start. But I did know something. I did know that at least one of the other instructors had been having an affair with Mrs. Bulpitt.

The hell, you say. Really. No accounting for taste. I wouldn't touch her with a ten-foot pole. But speaking of Poles...

It was a Pole who was seeing Mrs. B. OK. I'll admit it. I sort of knew Mrs. Bulpitt had a thing for Iggy. At least, that was the water-cooler gossip. It had to be a coincidence that the cops has asked me if I had ever been to Poland. Ignatz was supposed to be on holiday there this very minute. What in heavens name would Italy have to do with Ignatz, or me with Poland? It was a muddle.

***

We get a lot of foreign students. French, Spanish, German, Polish. A few Italian, the odd American. No Canucks, though; Canadians and Aussies can make direct transfers of their home licence for a British one. Too bad, really. I hear Canucks have a really good sense of humour. I wouldn't mind meeting some.

And they are polite.

"How do you get 200 Canadians out of a swimming pool?" I asked Chloe.

Silence.

"You say, 'Would everyone mind please leaving the pool now, please?'"

Silence. Followed by, "Do you have any other ethnic jokes stashed in your gormless little head that you want to tell me?" she asked.

No. Because I only knew a few about Poles, and I was still thinking about Poles, but I was thinking (mainly) more acceptable things. For example, I had found it tough to know what Poles are thinking. Maybe it is all that time they spent being stepped on by the Cossacks from next door and then later by the Master Race from their southern border. It always amused me that both Otto von Bismarck (arch-conservative architect of Germany's 19th century army) and Karl Marx (communist) were both Prussians. This means that although the Germans claim them—having swallowed up war-mongering Prussia which casts a certain light on Germany, yah?—they were really Polish.

###

Political Correctness is cultural Marxism. It is Marxism translated from economic into cultural terms. It is an effort that goes back not to the 1960s and the hippies and the peace movement, but back to World War I. If we compare the basic tenets of Political Correctness with classical Marxism the parallels are very obvious." And both are totalitarian ideologies.—Bill Lind, "The Origins of Political Correctness," *Accuracy in Academia* **website, Feb. 5, 2000.**

###

So maybe those jokes about the all-expense-paid four-day, seven-night trip to Poland to see the book in their library aren't true. Who knows? Trying to cast a race or a people in one mould or another is fruitless, the proof of which is that it was our Polish instructor who was reputed to be having an affair with Gertrude Hermione Dorcas Bulpitt. I can't imagine either von Bismarck nor Marx would have considered that an admirable thing for a Polish-Prussian-German to do.

Note that I said *reputed.* I personally didn't know anything about it. And Ignatz is actually a pretty decent guy, and a darn good instructor, which would give the lie to that Polish humour stuff, in which I indulge, but only because, at base, I love everybody. No, really. I do. I just can't see a guy going around being an obvious New Age flake. Alf Garnett seems more my style. (For American readers, think Archie Bunker. *All in the Family* was copied from a British show—yup, really—called *Till Death Do Us Part.* But the patriarch was pretty much a carbon copy.)

Frankly, I couldn't see Ignatz and the distaff Bulpitt. But Ignatz got on well with everyone, unlike me, so I couldn't imagine why anyone would start that rumour. Still, he had taken the past week off, said he had to fly to Poland suddenly to see about moving his dear old mama to a nursing home or something.

Nah. I was thinking that, but it's daft.

"There is really nothing to do but go about your business until the police know more," Chloe told me. "And you may never hear from them again, or you might. If you do, I'd say get some counsel…."

I jumped out of my skin. Was she saying that I needed a barrister on call in case I ended up in the dock?

"What happened to that peaceful yoga instructor I once knew and loved?" Chloe asked. "Calm down. It's just common sense. You know, that stuff you're supposed to be teaching people week after week."

That was common sense *in traffic*, I told her. She laughed. Common sense is common sense. Except when you're in the middle of something as nonsensical as having stinking, dripping, decomposing bodies show up in a learner car and being hauled into the cop house and grilled—well, OK, left alone for long periods and questioned—repeatedly, by two different cops asking the same questions, for a good part of the night. Didn't sound so bad that way…except if you then realize that left only a little bit of the night that I wasn't being grilled….

But she was right. And it was time I got home to my wife and faced the music. Perhaps there would be some leftovers from the meal of two nights back. Maybe she'd let me into the bedroom. Heck, maybe she'd let me into the house. I couldn't help comparing, but suddenly I couldn't understand how I had let The

Cobra slip away, and ended up with Lucretia Borgia. All that stuff about how lovely my wife is when she slithers off the sofa after I've been a crashing jerk? I was compensating, trying to find something good to say about her. The truth is, my wife drives me crazy, crazier than the others did. Maybe that's the charm. Maybe she's Lucretia Borgia and Sophia Loren and the Madonna all rolled into one. (No, not Madonna. THE Madonna.)

Did I say that? Did I think that? I didn't know. What I did know was that I had a busy week ahead. Some of us work seven days a week, and I had just cancelled two days. Those punters were going to be clamouring for makeup lessons, and there were only so many hours in a day. I hated teaching some learners after dark; daylight was bad enough. But then you get the ones like Michael, who told me he could drive already but just wanted to brush up before his first lesson. He could start the car, move it forward, and keep it off the kerb. Just. But when we got out on the roads, he asked me to cover the rear-view mirror.

"Why?" (Are you beginning to notice most of my questions are one or two words? Obviously, I've had to limit my vocabulary to address the audience before which I usually perform, moronic learner drivers. And Bulpitt.)

"Because I can see things moving in it and it confuses me."

Ba-da-bing. And it went downhill from there. You can imagine how much I wanted him on the roads after dark. "Can I just turn off the headlights, Mr. Barker? Seeing those people crossing the road confuses me." Yup. Sure. And I REALLY don't have an ulcer. Yet.

I don't really have to work at all, as long as I stay married to Wife No. 4. So why seven-day weeks? Why put up with the Michaels of the world? Have you seen my wife? Seriously, she's lovely to look at. It's all me. I just can't spend time with myself.

No hobbies, remember? And I can't spend time with her, because then I'm reminded of my inadequacies. I mean, what man would feel adequate in the presence of a Renaissance murderess, a hot Italian actress and the mother of the son of God, and rich as Croesus to boot? And no, I don't need to see a psychiatrist. I'm busy emoting for you, so I can't see how I could have any deep, dark secrets that need to be revealed. What you see is what you get. Just me. Like it or lump it. Buyer beware.

Finally, there was no help for it. I had to leave Chloe and return to the Bay of Naples.

SEVEN

Que Sera, Sera

I didn't have to open the door to know that an Alitalia flight had landed in my front garden. I could hear the tarantella booming through the open window which was letting out all the cigarette smoke. I could hear the cousins (lord, how many of them had come?) arguing loudly about whether England had any authentic Italian food or not. We do have Pizza Hut. I had pointed that out once. I had discovered just how frightening blank stares could be on the otherwise animated faces of dark-skinned, velvet-eyed Italians.

I could hear female voices, several of them. I thought I heard Aunt Rosalie, because somebody sounded like Andy Devine, the late American gravel-voiced cowboy actor, and that had to be Rosie. I called her that. Rosie that is, although calling her Andy had occurred to me. I just didn't want my face rearranged. I like the way my somewhat large nose is in the middle...and no, you cannot call it a bulbous honker. I liked my green eyes opening and closing at will, and I didn't want the cheekbones to go away. They were my best part.

I was always glad I had cheekbones, especially after I saw that comedian who used to be on *Mock the Week* a lot. He's a funny guy, and I think women might like him with his curly black hair and easy grin. But the man has no cheekbones. I swear, from his eyes to his chin, it's one flat plane. I knew people in my wife's extended family could do that to a person via the Sicilian Facial

Rearrangement Program, no appointment necessary. But still, I just couldn't help calling the matriarch of that family Rosie.

She hated it. "Do I look like a Rosie to you, chooch!" she would growl, slapping me on the back of my crew cut skull. Chooch is Italian-American slang for jackass, dummy...stuff along those lines. It comes form the Italian ciuccio; as my wife so elegantly told me once, a chooch is one who, "against his better judgment, acts inappropriately. In short, you." Americans do NOT sugar-coat their opinions. Not even Italian-Americans.

"Sure you look like a Rosie, you sweet thing," I'd reply, attempting to get my arms around her. This was a slapstick routine that had become part of family lore, such as it was. I had repeated it once, and then it became part of my schtick regarding Rosalie. It always reminded me of the title of that play, *Your Arms Too Short to Box With God*. The play was based on the book of Matthew in the Bible. I only know that because of teaching at the University of the Deeply Held Belief that There Is a God Who Lives on Cloud and Has a Flowing White Beard. OK. That's not its real name either. But when an experience scars one as badly as teaching at that sinkhole for native human intellect, one tries to deflect it. At least that's what my shrink told me once when I was sunk in despair on his deep, comfy sofa trying to figure out why the University of Cockamamie Christian Fantasies had not granted me tenure, and I'd had to go and actually look for work.

But no, I don't need a shrink now. I just need a way out of this mess, a way to find out who killed Mrs. Bulpitt, and a way to go back to enjoying my life as I had when I was....when I was....OK. So I have never enjoyed my life. Maybe I need a new job now, too.

Anyway, Rosalie and I played the name game every time we saw each other—must be five or six times now—and it never got old. She loved to have a pale face to swat, and I loved to annoy my wife who hated me to make her Italian relatives look so Italian by comparison to my very angular Anglo-Saxon self. I loved it.

"Rosie," I yelled entering the house, and the floor shook.

"Stupido," she croaked, trundling past the sofa where three sets of female legs in fishnet tights stuck out, probably to show off their high-heeled sneakers...or whatever one calls those things are that look like high-top rugger shoes with door stops pasted on the back. She hit me. She hugged me. I began to gasp, and she let me go. I was still gasping. By the way, stupido is pronounced STEWpido, emphasis on stew. I tripped over the hem of a humongous cashmere overcoat draped over a chair. Big Rosie's. He never went anywhere without it, winter or summer. I guess you never knew when you might need to cover a bullet hole or two, or maybe he just liked the look, the huge long coat—below knee-length, like in old-time gangster movies—always open, always just laid across the shoulders like a royal cape. It had a fur collar. Not ermine. I don't think.

I motioned my wife to open all the windows wider. The smoke from the American menthol cigarettes was choking the life out of whatever lung cells I had left since their last visit, only a few months back. Do they hire a whole plane, or what? I asked myself, realizing that I was slipping into Brooklyn Italian patois. It happened every time they came. Maybe it was the gravy. To Italian-Americans, tomato sauce is gravy. Don't ask me why; I'm still wondering why they eat a luncheon meat named something in Italian that I've been told translates to Dead Donkey. There's another story there, about a donkey. But it comes later. I have to tell this tale the way it happened. No tying up loose ends before time; no trying to make it freaking literary. Remember, I no longer teach at the University of the Holy Grail Sought by Three Wise Men and Found by Shepherds and Asses…darn, there I go again. Ass. Donkey. Tying it up. And no, that's not its name either. But it's near Christmas as I write this, so the symbols are cramming my head.

Anyway, I had to count heads. It sounded like an entire Sons of Italy meeting was going on out on the deck. I heard at least four male voices. So, I sneaked a peek through the kitchen curtain, and there they were, the entire Melanzane family, plus one.

Who was the extra? I knew Rosalie's husband, Big Rosie. I swear, that's his name. Maybe that's why Rosalie hates for me to call her Rosie; it confuses her and she thinks I want her husband. But I know the difference. His boobs are a bit smaller, his stomach a bit bigger, his voice a bit higher, and he also has no hair. On his head. That's all I know. About Big Rosie's hair. But at least his follicular condition keeps dandruff from getting on his silk suits. Always a silk suit. And always, in the buttonhole, a rose. Or at least, every time I had seen him. Even now, standing on my deck. Standing on a freaking deck in East Anglia, in a semi-detached house (who knows what the neighbours think? Who cares.) Standing there, yelling back and forth with the other three. Biff was looking soulful, hiding under the table, away from the smoke, away from the noise.

"I'm telling you, Pop," Big Rosie's son, Double R, answered. "There is nothing we can do until what's missing is found."

Missing? Was that Mrs. Bulpitt they were discussing? Nah…..it couldn't be. How would they even know about that?

While I was panicking, there was silence. All I could hear for a few seconds was four men exhaling smoke, thankfully outdoors. Later, I would get little notes from my closest neighbour asking me to curtail the habits of my guests, that she was hacking up phlegm and had to miss a day at her health club because of my inconsiderate friends, and so on and on and on. What a pain. Still, she was quiet and I just tore up her whiney notes.

Then Big Rosie spoke. "I hate to see a woman so miserable. I promised her father, god rest his soul, that I would make sure she was happy, that his money was being well spent."

Silence. They WERE talking about me. I always thought Double R liked me. Double R was because his name was Robert (Roberto) Roderick (Roderigo) Melanzane and his parents were both with R....maybe it should have been Quadruple R, but I don't think that crowd could handle the word. Most people called him Double R, but I teased him once, by calling him Bobby Rod, the sort of nicknames they use in the American South. He didn't hate it immediately, which had been my self-destructive intention, so I told him about the cannoli and how rednecks don't know from cannoli (slipping into the Yiddish usage I learned from a former wife)...and now he hates it. Good. Chalk one up for the British team. Minus one for Bobby Rod. In any normal culture, he'd have been called Roddy anyway. Normal being defined—by me—as Brit or Mick.

At that moment, I figured I needed to make a hasty retreat, but then the fourth guy, the one I didn't know, spoke up. "Maybe we need a fixer, you know, like the Jewish people have. I read about it once, a book by Bernie Mallamudda."

Head slap on the fourth guy's Neanderthal forehead from Cousin Tommy.

"Bernard Malamud, you jadrool. But at least you got the story right. I didn't even know you could read."

I didn't know any of them could read. OK. That's overstating the case. But *The Fixer*? This is a story about weltschmertz on a global scale by a global author. The "fixer" wasn't the kind of fixer a Brooklyn Italian connected with that organization that doesn't exist (according to the Italian-American anti-defamation league, or something.) Malamud's character literally fixed stuff, broken stuff. Then he got arrested on suspicion of murder (OK, that makes sense with this crowd), and in jail he does a lot of thinking. He even forgives his ex-wife. (Don't get any ideas! She's still The Cobra. Maybe Cobra-ette, maybe even garter snake if she could get me through this problem, I thought.)

Because I still have a problem. I had never been hauled into the police station before. Cripes, they actually suspected me of offing whatever—whomever—was in the back of the learner car. Or maybe they didn't. Maybe The Cobra was right and they really only wanted to see what I knew to help them connect the dots.

My other problem I got at the moment (see how easily I can slip into Brooklynese grammar and usage? All from being around my wife and this crowd, even though my wife speaks correct American English, to use an oxymoron)…anyway, the other problem is: Do I just go out and offer them a "brewski"? I don't know if Italian-Americans use that term, actually, but at least it's American, maybe some brownie points for me…. Or do I just go back inside and hang with Rosalie, the three stoogettes and my wife?

What, I want to be a jadrool? Or worse, a nancy. No. So I decided to go out on the deck.

"Hey, Big Rosie," I say, crossing the deck, trying to give him the locker room rap on the upper arm, being repulsed by Double R getting in between. I guess he was afraid I'd feel the piece under Big Rosie's armpit. How did he get the things into the UK, I'd like to know. Or maybe he just had a connection locally and picked one up on arrival, like a rental car. Speaking of which, I never knew they rented Mafia staff cars at Heathrow, but those two things in front of the house could be called nothing else.

They were almost matching 1988 Mercedes 560SELs, except one didn't have tinted windows. Tinted windows are a must for a Mafia staff car, so the cops can't see who's in there. I figure the ladies drove the untinted one so they could show off their *Married to the Mob* hairdos and earrings. (By the way, *Married to the Mob* is a great movie, especially if you need a training film to deal with the sorts of problems my wife's family presents. I always think maybe I look like Matthew Modine.)

Both of the cars were dark grey; they could disappear on the street. They had roomy interiors. They have to. A lot of business is done at gunpoint in the back of a Mafia staff car. And they have really big boots, good for stashing drugs or bodies. Oy vay. What am I thinking?

I didn't really have time to think because before I could even get a pleasant greeting out of my mouth, Big Rosie had jumped on me.

"Whatsa matta wid youse," he bellowed. "You can get your ass in the slammer over what, a fucking murder, and bring trouble on my favourite niece? I sent her to New York University why? So you could make her into some kinda gun moll or something? Jadrool." He flicked his baby cigar over the railing and into the garden. I could see it smouldering; I hadn't done much gardening lately, there hadn't been much rain, and the brown dying leaves under the hostas in the dark corner were dry enough to catch fire.

Please catch fire! I implored them silently. I need a diversion from Big Rosie's interrogation. I had enough of that, already.

EIGHT

Secret Agent Man

From my mouth to God's ears. I got a diversion all right. Just at that moment, one of the stooges screamed, "Ohmygawditshere."

Rosalie punched open the back door and gave Big Rosie and Double R looks that would raise the dead. They both went running into the house, yelling for Tommy and the jadrool to warm up the cars, they had to get Mrs. Jadrool to the hospital pronto. She was having a new little Melanzane right now. Right *now*!

Well, it wouldn't be a Melanzane. I had never seen her before in my life, so I knew she wasn't Double R's wife. Not Cousin Tommy's either. Both of them were perched on the sofa. Well, had been perched. Now they were out the door like a burlesque routine, trying to squeeze both those rumps through it at the same time, Rosalie bringing up the rear so to speak with the Little Mama about to drop another squalling bambino into the overcrowded World Soup. The Little Mama had to be with the fourth guy. Who *was* the fourth guy? So far, I guessed I would have to call him Jadrool, if I called him at all.

I was actually hoping, as the getaway commenced with a lot of door banging, head slapping and "Madon'" yelling, that my wife wasn't going with them. I wanted to apologize to her, if she'd let me, for not coming home. And I wanted to ask her who that fourth guy and the mummy-to-be might be. And I wanted a large, large helping of the luganica she had on the stove. The smell was driving me crazy.

The guests must have brought the sausages with them. I have never been able to find them for sale in England. I *think* they're called luganica. Pork (so why should they be hard to find in England? We have tons of pork) and garlic and fennel seeds and a little hot pepper. My wife has even made some at home, just as patties and not in a sausage casing, but the real thing is a lot better.

How did they get them into the country? Was customs asleep? I thought sausages were agricultural products, and as such, not eligible to be imported by ordinary people. Well...the Melanzanes were hardly ordinary people, but you know what I mean. So how did they get them in? Don't ask. I just eat the sausages; I don't interrogate the sausage-bearers.

My wife stayed.

"I'm sorry," she said. "I know. I forgive you. But I went a little nuts and I called Rosalie and before I know it, the whole clan is here. Plus that other couple. And now there's going to be one more. How did they let her on the plane? They usually won't let pregnant women on when they are that *enciente*?"

I told you my wife had a university degree. No dummy.

"Did you see her? How could they tell where fat ended and baby started?" I asked. My wife gave me one of those "don't start your crap" looks, so I continued. "I mean, it's a wonder she didn't have to pay for two seats. Hey...how did they get here so fast anyway?"

"Don't ask," said my wife. "I mean, I didn't ask. I don't think I want to know. It's like the tooth fairy. They just come, and if you're lucky, they go away silently and leave a little something under your pillow."

"Only if you leave them a little part of yourself," I said.

My wife glared.

"I mean like a tooth," I said, although she knew I knew she knew it wasn't what I meant. Anyway, tooth or nose hair, I didn't think I had any spare parts I wanted to donate to the cause of getting rid of my wife's extended family.

"They aren't...," she started, and then began to cry.

This was a new side to my wife, one I had not seen before. I always thought she was wedded to her Italian family from Brooklyn and New Jersey and the idea of some people "sleeping with the fishes" if they crossed Big Rosie. Not that I think Big Rosie is a don, not at all. Why would I think that? He's in construction, sure. And they have lots of cement. And also, he lives in one of the very oldest Brooklyn Italian neighbourhoods and also has a summer home on a canal on the south shore of Long Island. He has a big boat. Really big. I've heard. I've never been on it. But apparently, you can load it down with stuff—booze, people, cement overcoats—and it still floats high enough above the water line not to attract the attention of the U.S. Coast Guard. And he wears silk suits that LOOK like silk suits, none of that Savile Row understatement. Plus, he fancies them up with a rose in the lapel every day. Every day a fresh one, like Dave the Dude had to have from Apple Annie, the bag lady in *Pocketful of Miracles*. (OK, so I'm an old movie junkie. But that one was great, with Bette Davis as Apple Annie, Glenn Ford as Dave the Dude and the late, great Peter Falk—Columbo!—as a minor hood named Joy Boy.) But do I think Big Rosie is a don? Put it this way: I think whatever Big Rosie wants me to think, so he's simply the well-off owner of a construction company that gets very few contracts, but keeps guys employed anyway.

I didn't understand the crying. I was a little upset that my wife was being so....what's that New Age term? Right, vulnerable. She was acting vulnerable, completely out of character. Out of

role play? I began to wonder if my attitude toward my wife
wasn't scripted, like all the remarks the driving examiners are
supposed to use when they are testing a licence candidate. I had
to derail both her tears and my train of thought, so I reminded my
wife that she had called Big Rosie this time anyway. "What was I
supposed to do?" she wailed. "You were arrested,...

"I was not arrested. I was helping the police with their
enquiries."

"As I said, you were arrested...."

I wasn't going to get any quarter here, she was too upset, but
it wasn't doing my mental state any good, so I got up to pour
some of the wine I saw on the table, a big bottle among the
abandoned glasses, another bottle, ashtrays...where did the
ashtrays come from? Did they bring them? Yeah, they must have
brought them. I know I didn't have one from Krakow. From
WHERE? Krakow? OK. I'm cracking up. That's in Poland. So
all of a sudden, Italy and Poland are top of mind with me. More
accessible than TV adverts with little talking meerkats in them.
Meerkats from Poland. Well, no, Russia. I was getting carried
away. Coincidence, that's all.

"You were arrested and then you didn't come home and you
waited so long to phone."

"Half six?"

"I was up all night, worrying." I could scarcely believe it. I
really didn't think she cared. Usually when I asked her what she
had made for dinner, she replied, "A booking at Palermo
Ristorante." Could a woman who only cooked for you about half
the time, if you were lucky, be counted on to miss you when you
were swooped upon by dirty coppers and held incommunicado? I
might have to rethink the relationship.

"Shelf, I didn't know what to do. I was so upset. So I called Rosalie, to talk. Just to talk. I can call her anytime on Skype, and she answers. I don't think she sleeps much, really. But I guess she was upset. I didn't know she cared about you, either. Anyway, she told me go to sleep, they'd be right over. That was two days ago. The first night you were gone. I called her the second night, too. I got the voice mail, so I figured they were in transit.

"OK. But why did she bring the whole crowd? If he wanted to, Big Rosie could have whacked me all by himself. Hell, he could sit on me and I'd....

"Shelf, you make it very difficult even for a patient woman to love you, you know that?

I was abashed.

I looked down and murmured sheepishly.

"I don't know why they brought that whole crowd. I guess Rosalie figured it would help if I had my cousins around. So I guess she grabbed Double R, who grabbed Cousin Tommy and then they all came over."

"What about the other ones, the preggers broad and her dude?"

"No, they were here already. In England. What, you think someone 10 months pregnant is allowed on an airplane? It might be a bomb under there."

I always thought they didn't let wildly pregnant women fly because of possible damage to the baby, or maybe she'd end up spreading her legs in the aisle if the pressure changes opened the birth canal. That would be so inconvenient, I always thought, because then they couldn't get the pay-per-drink beverage cart down the aisle. I figure his accountants told Sir Richard not to let preggers broads on because he might go broke without that extra four pounds fifty per head for firewater that they don't give you on planes anymore so you can forget you are squeezed into a germ-laden tube hurtling through space and doing god-knows-what to your internal organs, biological clock, and so forth. Make that six pounds fifty; the economy is tanking, which means you can always get more shekels out of punters for booze. Helps ease the pain, which is what my second glass of wine was doing, now that the gulped-down first glass had hit behind my belt buckle.

I didn't expect the doorbell to ring. My wife and I both jumped.

"Miracle!" I said.

"No, just the doorbell," said my wife, rising to open it and peering through the nicotine-smudged front window. "Oh." Disdain crept out of her pores.

For reasons I cannot fathom, my wife always disliked Miracle. I think she thought Miracle and I had something going, but she was wrong. Miracle is just an amusing human being, and since most of the people I deal with are as bull-headed as Bulpitt or as terrifying as 9 out of 10 learner drivers, I don't see the harm.

She looked awful, Miracle did. Like she'd been through a driving test with that horrific examiner in Cornwall who gave people instructions to do something illegal and then failed them, nastily, when they refused to do it. I had seen the results of that, and someday...well, someday will never come. There are good bureaucrats and bad ones. I'm not going to waste any energy tracking that guy down and punching out his lights. We are lucky where I live; the examiners are mostly good.

Of course, having a few rotters dotted around the nation did make for a good income for companies like ours. Companies that take on new drivers sent to psychiatry by the shenanigans of some of the driving examiner, the ones that were truly pathological, like that Cornwall guy. People who were tested and failed by them tended to want to go anywhere, spend anything not to risk another encounter with the devil in a bureaucrat suit. So perhaps I shouldn't complain. Still, I do have some ethics…and abusing learner drivers is just plain wrong.

Usually, it is the driving examiners being subjected to abuse. "Five examiners suffered physical attacks and 209 reported being verbally abused as stress got the better of candidates, according to Driving Standards Agency statistics obtained by windscreen repair firm Autoglass," according to a May 5, 2011 article, "Hundreds of learner drivers hurt behind the wheel during their tests" in the *London Evening Standard*.

Then again, learner drivers abusing instructors is just plain wrong, and is likely to cause a lot more trouble than the odd rotten driving examiner. I doubt I'm alone in having had one learner who liked to take her hands of the wheel and put at least one of them on my crotch. And no, I didn't like it. What are these people thinking? What sort of tactics are used to raise them? Is there a supernanny for teens? There should be.

Before you decide I think instructors are all saints, I don't. One of them liked to put his hand on his female students' private parts. The brother of one fondled student found out about it and, instead of beating the guy to a pulp, frogmarched him to a Cash Point and had him empty his bank account. I don't know if it cured him, but it was a nice turnabout without getting the cops involved.

***

I led Miracle to the sofa, handed her a glass of wine, sat in the chair my wife had vacated and waited. It wasn't long before

Miracle began to talk, and talk, and talk, and talk. It was at least two hours before she even took a breath. What did she say?

I'll paraphrase, and I'm leaving out the Italian patois. I'd be typing until my next divorce.

"Mr. Bulpitt called me at home and insisted I come into the office," she said. "When I got there, he insisted I help him find everything ever

written about or filed for or about you.

"Me?"

Both my wife and Miracle rolled their eyes. I feared they were bonding.

"Mr. Bulpitt was nasty about it. He just smirked every time something with your name on it came up. If it had anything about money on it, he just gloated," she said.

"Then he made me look on every hard drive on every computer and do a search for your name. It took all morning. But there wasn't much to find, just emails from students booking lessons or thanking you. There were one or two that complained."

My eyebrows went up, and I reflexively pointed to myself. My wife and Miracle both got that female expression down right, right away—the one where one side of the mouth pulls up and the eyes roll. That one.

"Mr. Bulpitt's mood did not improve at all," Miracle said. "He was even nastier after I told him I absolutely didn't think you and Mrs. B had been lovers. He's lucky I didn't laugh in his face. I can't think of anything more laughable. You and Mrs. Bulpitt? I mean, any woman might seek a lover, but you?"

"Hey…"

"Come on, Shelf," my wife said. "You don't have affairs. You have divorces and remarriages."

"So anyway, when Mr. Bulpitt asked if you and his wife had ever been naughty together, I answered him, 'Only the once'." She and my wife were rolling about laughing. I didn't even bother to comment or object.

"I was sorry I said it as soon as it was out of my mouth. I should know better than to try to make a joke with Mr. Bulpitt. I'm afraid I got you in trouble."

I raised my eyebrows.

"He ran out of the room and I figured he was going to the police station to report that you were his wife's lover."

What she actually said was, "He's-a run outta da room and I think he's a going to da police-a station wid a report dat you done-a done his-a wife. I know you dinna done-a nothin'. I taught he woulda known-a that. But he's a stoopeed....an' I jus...."

I liked the way she said that, that I done-a done his wife, which I didn't done. It just sounded funny, and I laughed, although both my wife and Miracle—together—scowled.

What was going on here? There seemed to be entirely too much female camaraderie here. How does that happen? That women go from mortal enemies to bosom buddies in less than the time it takes to cook a goose. Goose. My goose. It was cooked, alright. If not by the cops, then by a pair of women ganging up on me. I hoped it wasn't going to be the start of an epidemic.

Still, I composed my face, eliminating the shock at seeing my wife warm up to Miracle, and told Miracle it was all right. Bulpitt wouldn't have known a joke if he heard it in plain English, never mind whatever accent Miracle was doing at the time. The cops had already grilled me once, and I could take it if they did it again. But they wouldn't, I assured her. I didn't know this, but it sounded good, anything to calm the poor girl down,

Nicky McBride

not to mention getting her out of there before the Comedia dell'Arte returned. Or my wife decided we should adopt her.

This was all I needed. Miracle crying on the sofa, my wife making soothing noises and bringing her some chamomile tea to calm her nerves, and the entire Melanzane family gathered around making fun of me behind (they thought) my gullible British back.

Fortunately, the Melanzanes were all at the hospital with Mrs. Jadrool awaiting the arrival of a little moron. Moron Jadrool. Sounded good to me. Maybe I should suggest it? But wait; their last name isn't Jadrool, I thought. Maybe they are Melanzanes, just distant cousins I had never met. But my wife didn't know them either. In fact, since no one had had time to introduce me properly to the Jadrool or Mrs. Jadrool, they could be anyone. So maybe I could suggest Jerkoff Jadrool. Sure. And maybe I should whack my own knees. The one thing? These Brooklyn and New Jersey Italians can't take a joke. Not at all.

Once I had told them my favourite Italian joke, *The Italian Who Goes to New York.*

> "When he arrives in his hotel, he checks the room and finds things are missing. So he calls the hotel desk and says, 'There'sa no sheet on my bed.'
>
> "The girl say, 'You sheet on the bed, you sonamabeech, I keela you.'
>
> "Then he goes out to a restaurant and orders a meal. While he's waiting, he notices he is lacking utensils. 'There'sa no fock onna table,' he says.
>
> The waitress says, 'You no fock onna table, you sonamabeech. I'ma keel you.'

When the meal arrives, he notices something he ordered is missing. The plate contains only a steak, and no vegetables. 'There'sa no piss onna my plate,' he says.

The answer: 'You piss onna da plate, you sonamabeech, I'ma keel you'."

"The Italian say I'ma go backa to Italy, where we gotta sheet ona bed, piss onna plate anna fock onna table."

And so it went. And no one laughed. I had always thought it was just in a film that Marlon Brando was so mirthless as the godfather. After all, Robert DeNiro was pretty mirthful in *Analyze This*. I much preferred his version of the capo to Brando's. But what do I know? I never had to whack somebody to make a living, never even wanted to despite my obvious negative attitudes much of the time.

That was about to change.

NINE

When the Moon Hits Your Eye Like a Big Pizza Pie

It was amazing, but I found I was actually in love with my wife. (What? You thought I was going to tell you about my sudden desire to whack someone? Not yet.)

My wife went to the kitchen and came back with some fresh wine glasses; she had taken away the disgusting smelly ashtrays and dumped the contents in the trash at the same time. Thankfully, she left the stinking objects in the kitchen, filled with soapy water. That wasn't because she wanted to make them easier for her to clean later. She did this because she wouldn't wash them. She wouldn't touch them. I had to clean them up after her family, but at least filling them with soapy water put an end to the stench until got to them. Anyway, when she came back into the room, she looked concerned. As I said before, she wasn't concerned that I might lose my income; it was peanuts next to her stash anyway. So she must have been concerned about me.

She offered Miracle some wine.

"Miracle, you look a little peaked. Have you had lunch?"

"No, Mistera Bulapeet wasa stilla going at it duringa lunchatime, and then I wanted to come-a here and see Shelf...."

OK. It wasn't all wine and roses yet. My wife got that pinched "how nice" look on her face. But she battled through it, and the helpful, angelic beatific smile returned in an instant.

"Let me get you something to eat," she said. "We have some nice luganica and ciabatta bread."

My wife went to the kitchen again, and I went and opened the second bottle of wine sitting unopened on the table. I still had some from the open bottle in my glass; and my wife decided to abstain since she had no idea what might go on when the Melanzanes returned, or whether she might have to go to the hospital (why? she didn't even know these people). But my wife is not stupid, as I said, and sometimes you need your wits about you to deal with Big Rosie. Plus she's really good at planning ahead. Me? I live for the moment. I just wish more of those moments were good.

I sort of wished my wife had brought me some of that luganica, too. My eating had been irregular, to say the least, the last few days. And I wished I had taken some of the second bottle of wine. It was homemade, or so the label said. One of those cute things with grape leaves on it and a space for the winemaker to write his or her name, only none was written. Who cared? But how did they get THAT in through customs? Anyway, some of that homemade stuff was potent, and I would not have minded drinking a bit, passing out and having a good sleep, the first one I'd have had in days.

Miracle did pass out. Correction: Miracle went into a coma. At least that's what it looked like. She was barely breathing.

"Shelf, Shelf," my wife screamed. "This is more than I can handle. I was just warming up to her. What is wrong with her? Did she take drugs or something before she got here? A little glass of Big Rosie's wine? No, it shouldn't do that. Not unless there's something wrong with her. What are we going to do?"

Or unless there was something wrong with the wine, I thought but didn't say. Big Rosie did seem to have it in for me, and there was the stuff I had overheard....

I dialled 999, and almost before my wife could get her makeup touched up and Miracle's skirt pulled down, the paramedics were in the house, stabilizing Miracle for a trip to the hospital. The same hospital where the Melanzanes and the Jadrools were engaged in waiting for their own miracle. And no, I had nothing to do with Miracle's skirt riding up, obviously. She had just sort of slumped over and then slid down the sofa onto the floor, so her mini was up around her…umm…lower regions. See, I'm not as randy and jerky a guy as you think. In fact, I'm quite a prude, really.

The paramedics loaded Miracle, my wife jumped in beside her, and I was left to follow in a car with a big red L on it, front and back. So there I was, weaving through traffic and doing daft things, like mounting the kerb (for some examiners, an automatic fail) and pulling into the box (ditto) and slicing through the last few seconds of a filter arrow until finally, a defender of the public safety pulled up behind me, lights swirling.

There I was, alone in an "L" car, so he must have figured I was some young boy racer and had stolen it. And besides, no instructor would allow a student to drive like that; god didn't make dual controls for fun.

"Mr. Barker, I have no idea what you think you were doing…." He began, looking over my licence.

"Following that ambulance to the hospital," I said. Why did I do that? Not say that. I said that because it is what I was doing. *Stupido*! I said to myself, channelling Rosalie.

I meant, why did I risk life, limb and a whopping great citation to keep up with the ambulance? I knew where they were going. The only reason I could think of was that I didn't want to walk in and face all those Melanzanes alone, especially as this had to constitute the second black mark against me as far as Big

Rosie was concerned. If I told them Miracle passed out—god, I hoped that's all she had done—after drinking Big Rosie's homemade hooch…I don't even want to think about it. I cannot tell him. Cripes, I suddenly realized. This copper had better hurry up and give me the damn ticket so I can go tell my wife not to tell Big Rosie. Tell him Miracle choked on a biscuit. Anything except that she took four or five sips of Big Rosie's vino and decided to imitate someone trying to take a dirt nap.

Not pleasant thoughts, any of them, although I had other fish to fry at the moment. I figured the peeler would run my name and come up with the fact that I had recently been helping his colleagues with their enquiries and haul me in again.

I was wrong, fortunately. He must have thought I was too *stupido* to do anything more stupid than what I had just done. I probably was that stupid. Imagine a driving instructor driving like an idiot, like a new father trying to get the little woman to the birthing room on time. Apparently that's what he thought, though, and that was good news for me, old as I am. Silver fox, that's what they call us old guys who become fathers for the first time. I didn't fancy myself a silver fox, but if he did, OK by me.

"Well, your wife's in good hands; she was alone and called the paramedics, right?" he said. (Whatever; I just smiled weakly at his assumption.) "I know how exciting this is—I've got nine kids myself and every one made my heart leap—but you want to be alive for the little one's birth, right? And you don't want to go to jail for killing someone with your car?"

I gasped.

"Calm down, Mr. Barker, please. You haven't killed anyone. I don't even think you took down any signage; if you had, I'd have to arrest you. He laughed, to show he was just being a nice, friendly sort of copper, community policing, health and safety, all that rot. If he didn't hurry up, my health and safety were going to be seriously compromised.

I took a deep breath. A really deep breath. When I let it out, it squeaked. Just the word arrest was enough to send me into myocardial infarct.

The cop looked at me oddly. "Being excited is OK, just pull over for a few minutes and calm yourself down. Then go on. But don't let me catch you doing anything like this again."

"No, officer."

Keep Calm and Carry On. Keep Calm and Carry On. Keep Calm and Carry On. I said it like a mantra for all of maybe two minutes at the side of the road, until I was sure Officer Daddy had gone on his way. In truth, underneath the external composure I finally achieved, the more appropriate signage would have been the opposite of that re-introduced 1939 motivational sentiment, meant to steady Old Blighty as war visited the nation. I was in much more a Now Panic and Freak Out mood.

The phrase "Keep Calm and Carry On" first appeared in 1939, on a now-familiar poster—white crown and lettering on a red ground—to build morale in Great Britain. Although 2,500,000 copies were printed, only a handful were distributed, awaiting fame decades later when the posters were rediscovered.— Researched by Prof. G. Barker

Whew. So I pulled out, drove slowly and carefully toward the hospital, and began to think. What WAS wrong with Miracle, anyway? Did she have a disease and shouldn't drink wine? What? Nah, she would have refused it. But then, would she be OK? Regardless of why she had passed out. At that point, my foot got twitchy on the pedal and I sped up again. A horrible thought: Was Officer Daddy lurking, waiting to get me again? No. He was gone, doubtless out after some useless prat—some boy racer, I should say—who had engaged in some old-lady tipping with his Clio.

TEN

Take It Easy

I parked, I walked, I vomited in the gutter.

I don't do that often, but just consider the recent events in my otherwise tawdry, boring life. To wit (I can say that, since I'm a former professor):

- A stiff—well, a dripper, or maybe two—was found in one of the learner cars belonging to the company I work for
- An apparently valuable diamond necklace belonging to the wife of my boss, with whom there is no love lost, was found in the mess
- I was invited to help the police with their enquiries
- I was so stressed, I looked to my ex-wife, The Cobra, for help
- She offered help; this may be the most stressful part of all. Don't people who once hated you often offer help when they figure your end is near? To sort of help it along? Am I getting paranoid?
- I returned home, expecting a chilly reception from the wife I have chronologically abused for two days, and get instead…
- A houseful of Italian relatives, who have landed on my doorstep, invaded my inner sanctum, and brought along…
- An additional paesan and Mrs. Paesan…or maybe it's really the Jadrool family…It could be a name.

It means cucumber, jadrool does. Odd things the Eye-tais use for insults.

- I experienced a sudden call to 999 because Mrs. Paisan a/k/a Mrs. Dopey a/k/a Mrs. Jadrool is 10 and a half months pregnant and about to produce another little cook/singer/hot movie star with jugs from heaven and lips from hell, or alternatively, another wise guy
- The appearance of Miracle to tell me Bulpitt was looking for dirt on me
- The passing out of Miracle because she drank some of Big Rosie's homemade wine
- Getting pulled over by one of East Anglia's finest who mistakenly thought I was rushing to join my wife who was giving birth.

You know what's the worst part of this, the thing that is most distressing underlying it all? My wife was prepared to be nice to me, and even to Miracle whom she loathes. What was going on? Maybe my ticket to ride the sky train had been punched and I was the only one who didn't know it.

Anyway, I headed right for the toilets so I could rinse my mouth before entering the fray. And it was a fray. The Melanzane family had made the emergency waiting room into a war council chamber. There must have been a few other people waiting, either to be seen or to collect someone else being seen by a doctor, but you couldn't tell by looking. It wasn't just that Big Rosie was big, Double R not much smaller, Cousin Tommy hefty as well and the Jadrool, a bantam next to them, was flitting around like a mosquito in September. Afraid to land because it might be his last fling, but yet filling all the otherwise unspoken for space incredibly annoyingly and emitting some sort of droning buzz from deep in his thoracic segment.

The women took up whatever space wasn't left by the men or invaded by the Jadrool. Rosalie was perched in the centre of one row of attached plastic conjoined chairs. (So sue me! It's a hospital; the term conjoined just seemed natural.) Rosalie had her massive arms stretched out over the seats beside her, her huge purse flung in front of another. She was muttering something under her breath. Italian. I have picked up some words, but long strings of stuff said sotto voce with hand gestures...well, I am a Brit, after all. What do you expect in only a couple of years?

Cousin Tommette was taking most of another row, stretching her legs out over a couple of seats and semi-reclining, like she was in a triple row all alone on a transatlantic flight, and watching a really engrossing movie.

Double R's wife was literally standing on a chair, poised to leap over, fishnet tights and all, and apparently smack Jadrool as soon as she could catch him. What for? Who knows? Who cares? This bunch of Brooklyn Italians is as likely to swat one of their own as an outsider; it's just they don't swat their own as hard. Maybe a broken finger, a little cut on the cheek...little stuff. Stuff any GP in their employ can easily fix up without having to report the surgery to some oversight committee someplace.

Behind the plexi-glass, a nurse had a phone to her ear. From the look in her eyes (fear) and the set of her mouth (anger), I figured she was calling security.

That I did not need, but I am fascinated by the voluble lifestyle of this Italian in-law family, so I failed to take another powder when I had the chance, back to the toilets for as long as it took. I was entranced by the scene; I figured I would escape the broken nose or dislocated shoulder, this time anyway, since whatever was going on with Jadrool could not possibly have anything to do with me, since I had just arrived.

It was a madhouse in there, a great sight for an old B-movie aficionado. It was bedlam, like the old version of Bethlehem Royal Hospital, the first recognized nuthouse on the planet (see, Britain is a nation of firsts!), and renowned for the noise and upheaval the inmates caused back in horse-and-buggy days. Bedlam…contraction of Bethlehem. Please excuse me for segwaying into professor mode.

As I stood frozen in front of the undulating tableau of loudly garbed, extravagantly gesturing, noisily arguing escapees from a Hieronymus Bosch painting, my wife came in and walked straight over to me. She had been busy in some deep recess of the building filling out forms for the still comatose Miracle. My wife seemed to be crying. Again.

What's with this? My wife doesn't cry. But she *was* crying. Just as uncharacteristically, I held her, stroked her hair and tried very hard to pretend we were not with—had nothing at all to do with—the Melanzane crowd when the rent-a-cop arrived.

I knew him. Did you know England is a small country? It is. And I knew Securi-Man. He had been one of my students a couple of years earlier. He was unforgettable, not because of his driving lessons, but because of the way he got famous not long after he got his licence.

I was tempted to clap him on the back in a friendly way and say, "How are you? Done any driving since your lessons?"

But I didn't. I didn't have to. Myron Lillicrap (I've changed his name to protect him from further media grief) dragged out the whole story, the one I had decided firmly against revealing—especially to the Melanzanes—when I greeted him. He was giggling like one of Gilbert and Sullivan's Little Maids from School as he trundled—brother, had he put on weight—over toward me.

"I can't believe it's you, Mr. Barker! I haven't even talked to you since that day I asked you about if you ever had another student like me." (Just so you know, no, I never had another student like him. They are all different. As Leo Tolstoy wrote in *Anna Karenina*, "Happy families are all alike; every unhappy family is unhappy in its own way." Apply it to driving students, and you've hit the jackpot.)

By this time, my wife was all ears, sidling away from me just a bit, but at least the crying was settling down.

Myron Lillicrap's path from walker to driver had not been a smooth one. Not the worst of them, but not without its hair-raising moments. Fortunately, he was fairly compliant when I was teaching him and simply did what I told him to do as best he could. Finally, after eight or nine months of weekly lessons he had the skills for passing the test, but his mentality? That was another story. But as mere instructors, we don't get to pass judgment on that, only on the required physical skills, before sending students for a driving test.

The first time Myron took his test, he failed because he ran right through a red light. He was otherwise engaged, looking behind him at an HGV closing fast, and forgetting to look ahead. Fail. Not epic, but fail just the same.

"I'm not upset," he told me at the time. "I did want to be better than average, but it's OK. I'll just take it again." Myron's attitude was remarkable, considering that he was already in his mid-forties, dabbled as drummer and singer in a hard-rock band, and was merely trying to get back into his real profession in catering—from his current job of carpenter/handyman. In Cornwall, where he was from and wanted to return to, he would need a car for catering; in big urban centres, not so much, which is why, early in his career, he had done catering by bus.

Don't ask, as Big Rosie would say. "Would you like some petrol soot or old lady's spewed mucus with your smoked salmon canapés?" I can just imagine the crap on that food after an hour or so in the London underground.

Myron was about on target for the statistics, in fact, by failing his first test. In the UK, on average, the first-time pass rate for new drivers hovers around 48 percent. Even with all the lessons. Indeed, I have a friend who swears that every third car on the road in Cornwall has a driving company logo and a big red L on it. It's not as cushy as she thinks, though. There's great competition for students, one reason my company does the five-day intensive course. But I take private students as well; my rep has gotten around and there are local driver wannabes who figure I'm patient and kind and they can drag out their pathway to driving nirvana for months, maybe years. So it's no wonder I often get to know my students better than my own family, which is, as noted, scanty to begin with and mainly loathes me as well.

The intensive course attracts a lot of students who don't want family and friends to know they're engaged in Britain's most frightful civilian pursuit, or who simply have the money to invest in getting the scariest test they'll ever take prepared for and over with pronto. Some do it for a new job that requires them to get a license and drive. Some do it because family members are sick of being family chauffeurs.

The second time Myron took the test was a bit different than the first, if no better. It all came down to Myron's inability to do two things at once: look around and use some sound judgment.

In this case, the examiner told him to turn left at a roundabout, but he had to go past a bus at a bus stop just before the roundabout. Just as he got to it, the bus began to pull away. Myron decided to race the bus to the roundabout in an attempt to get there first so he could turn left. He did manage it, but there was much screeching of brakes by the bus when it tried to let him get back in front of it.

Maybe in any other country, that wouldn't constitute an Epic Fail, but in Britain, Myron had violated at least two rules. First, one must never cause another road user (no, not driver, *road user*, which might include horses or wheelchairs) to alter course for one's convenience. Second, one must never undertake—that is, pass on the inside—another vehicle. Poor Myron was doomed from the start. So yes, it was an Epic Fail. Now that I think of it, maybe I'll write a drivers' manual someday. It will be easy to write, easier than telling you this story of the East Anglia Drippers. Because this is Great Britain, where manners are far more important than substance, it only needs one instruction:

Think of the most obsequiously polite manoeuvre you could possibly do in any given traffic situation, and do that.

Brilliant! I could write the same kind of book again for New York City. It would say:

Think of the most arrogantly obnoxious manoeuvre you could possibly do in any given traffic situation, and do that.

And the great and sovereign state of Georgia, USA:

Stop in the roadway without signalling to look at pigs rooting in their muddy field. No, really. No pigs? Then stop on a two-way street to talk with your friend coming in the other direction. Don't signal, don't move, and don't care.

The state of Maryland, USA, inheritor of Lord Calvert's Roman Catholic prudery and the ugliest state flag in the history of the world:

Never, under any circumstances, use your directional signal for any reason at all from now until the end of time life everlasting amen.

Road sense is the offspring of courtesy and the parent of safety.—Australian Traffic Rule, quoted in *Quotations for Special Occasions* by Maud van Buren

Interrupting my reverie, Myron had started telling the story of the donkey before I could stop him. My wife was enjoying it. She had heard it before, although only my take on it. But Myron had a whole new audience for a tale I'm sure he had told before, what with his penchant for performance on stage or at the stove, as the swarthy folk perked up their ears. Some—notably Mr. Dopey Jadrool —began inching toward us.

I came back to the present just as Myron was saying, "So I called Mr. Barker (gives me a big knowing grin) and asked, 'Have you ever had any of your pupils involved in an accident'?"

"Bloody hell," I said aloud.

"Yup, that's just what you did say, Mr. B....You said, "Bloody hell, what's happened?"

"Anyway, the gate was open, and first thing I know, the donkey is in the road in front of me. I couldn't stop. (Looking at me) Shelf, it was too close to me." And he got all teary-eyed, which might have been appealing in a *bona fide* cop, but not in a waddling, overweight rent-a-cop thankfully not licensed to carry a weapon. Myron seemed to be...well, unstable. On the other hand, it was a hospital, and they could shoot him up with mind- and mood-altering drugs if need be.

However, as the great American baseball star, Yogi Berra, used to say, it was déjà vu all over again. That's precisely what he said to me at the time, and although he had phoned to tell me the news, I heard the quaver in his voice and noted, at the time, the possibility that he was crying.

I guessed Myron's life hadn't gone forward much, then. In fact, unless he was moonlighting at his beloved catering, it wasn't. But he was certainly getting plenty of groceries from someplace. I hoped he wasn't driving a mini or Smart car. If he got in an accident, it would be like peeling a grape to get him out. The jaws of life? Forget that. They'd need a vegetable peeler, a really big one.

While I was in my reverie, Myron's doe-like eyes began to sprout tears, and suddenly, I thought I was going to have another crying dame on my hands. Oh, he's not a dame? I ask you: He's a cook, he drives like an old lady, he's crying in the middle of the Mini-Mafia Meeting at the Meathouse…and, what, you think he's straight? Look, I'm not homophobic, but I am a realist. As one of my students used to tell me, if you wonder, don't wonder. I was wondering. So I didn't wonder.

Anyway, Myron went on with his story, with several greasy bodies blotting out the sun, or at least the dim glow of the freaking useless Euro lights 12 feet above our heads, poking down from the cracked plaster that seemed still to be coated with years of cigarette smoke. And yes, one could once actually smoke in England, although not in recent memory and not in public places. That's fine with me, actually. I used to hate it when I had to tell my students not to smoke in class at the University of The Coming of the Next Rapture. No, that's not its real name either…and few of its students smoked because most regarded smoking as sinful. (You see, even a crack-brained fundamentalist university in the middle of mildly progressive England has some redeeming social value.)

Finally, Myron sniffed a few times, wiped the back of his hand across the region of his eyes, hitched up his trousers, shifted his holstered can of mace around (thank goodness they didn't issue firearms!), and continued.

"So I was just driving down the road. I was aware of donkeys beside the road, but the gate was always closed, so I didn't think anything about it. But then it was on my bonnet and I could see its face looking at me through the windscreen. It looked a bit frightened."

Myron stopped his narrative at that point and wiped at his eyes, again. Big Rosie wiped his eyes, too, drawing a silk handkerchief out of the breast pocket of the silk suit. Wow. I didn't know they were really supposed to be used. All the ones I had ever seen—and admittedly, that was just in hired monkey suits when I was obliged to be some poor wally's best man at a wedding in my youth—were little triangles of fabric sewn to a piece of stiff card stuck down into the pocket.

Rosalie wasn't crying. In fact, her mouth was scrunched up in distaste, whether from the idea of the poor donkey getting whacked by this jadrool, or because the jadrool was crying, or because Big Rosie was…no, not crying. I would never say that. But he was emotional, one might say.

"When I eventually stopped, the donkey flew off and landed in the road. The owner ran out of the house. She was a bit hysterical to be honest and called the police."

Big Rosie was shaking his head, dabbing again at his eyes. I heard him mutter something about a *poco asino*. I was fairly certain *asino* meant donkey; stood to reason. And no, I really haven't bothered to learn much Italian. No need, when English is the most well-known language on earth. It has 1.5 billion speakers, including those who claim it as first or second language, and those who claim it as their "foreign language." That's more even than ALL forms of Chinese put together. So why would a native speaker of English—me—bother to learn Italian? Most Italians knew some English. Well, four out of ten anyway. So really, in any situation with several people involved in Italy, there was almost bound to be an English speaker. As for the Italian-Americans, they didn't really speak either language fluently, unless you count the vocabularies for food, wine and whacking as in "terminate with extreme prejudice" as the American CIA, and for all I knew, MI5, would say it. For those, they spoke a sort of Italian. For everything else, there's a unique form of pidgin. I ask you: "Hey, whatsa matta for you dat youse gotta crud up my clean flaw wid ya muddy shews?" Is that supposed to be ENGLISH?

I had heard Myron's story at least half a dozen times, so I could afford to go off into some sort of reverie. But I could still retell it, etched as it was in the lesser cells of my brain where it cavorted with other gory scenes on the roads in England. Scenes like the one in which a student annoyed me once too often by calling the directional signals the tick-tock because of the noise they made. I didn't hit him. I didn't do anything, really, except float on a mental cloud of escapism, thinking of the guy trying to buy a car. "Does it have working tick-tocks?" he might ask. I'd like to be a fly on the wall. I had another nomenclature-challenged student who might have asked the sales person, "Does it go too slow so that people will be taking me over?" And he wasn't even Russian. Maybe we should opt for the American term for the same manoeuvre, passing. Overtaking is apparently too long a word for some more recently educate—if you can call it that—driving students.

Myron was rolling on, getting animated with hand gestures, almost as if he was an Italian himself. I never knew Myron had such talent as a mimic.

"The police came and helped me get the donkey off the road. Then I had to do a breathalyser. They smirked a lot," Myron said. This activity seemed to set off something among the Melanzane crowd. I can't imagine why; they aren't cops.

"The police decided it wasn't my fault as the gate was open, but I didn't have my license with me, so I had to go in the next day and show it to them. You know what the sergeant said to me when he saw my name?"

My wife looked at him quizzically.

"He said, 'Oh, so you are the Donkey Killer of Cornwall'."

The Melanzanes were all laughing. Not a lot, just a little. But they seemed to have warmed up to Myron, and calmed down from the state they were in before. Whew! I hadn't been looking forward to being swept up in the altercation. Escaping that possibility, I felt like innocent bystanders Victoria Grant and Toddy in *Victor, Victoria* when the gendarmerie busts up a fight in a Parisian café, and those two sloped out unseen.

But Big Rosie had seen me, and he was headed my way.

I could have killed someone. How did I go from mild-mannered driving instructor to buffoon of the century, putative murderer and lousy husband all in one go?

The one person I couldn't kill, though, was Big Rosie. He had finally made it over, under, around and through the muddle of his own family group plus one (Jadrool) and had an arm around my shoulder.

"You know, we didn't used to think much of you," he boomed so that the entire waiting room, the nursing staff behind the partition, the ambulance drivers outside and the kitchen help two floors below and a hundred yards north could hear it. "But this was good. This...this shows you really do offer a service to the world. You help clowns like this move out of the commercial kitchen where they touch the food people might eat and into a hospital where they can do less harm with their little mace canisters. Good for you," he said as he slapped my back. "Good for you."

Should I have told him that in England the term is "Good on ya?" Nah. I was beginning to want to live, even though I might have to contend with Melanzane bedlam from time to time. I wanted to live, that is, at least until the intern arrived and asked who was responsible for Miracle, and I said me.

That's when I started wanting to die.

ELEVEN

Only Love Can Break Your Heart

I wasn't really responsible for Miracle, not in the family sense. I had no idea if she had a family, except a sister of course, and the lunatic mother who had named her. I had no idea where they were or how to contact them. Maybe the hospital had found that information in her wallet.

I wasn't even her employer. But she had come to see me for a reason, a reason that impelled her to encounter my wife, for whom she had had no love either. So, yes, I guess I was responsible.

"We have saved the young woman's life," the intern said. "But we are going to need some information about where she was when she ingested the belladonna."

Thud. My wife hit the floor, the intern dropped his clipboard and ran to her, and I ran out the door. Big Rosie was running after me: I could tell by the way the ground shook. But I jumped a barrier and got into my car and out of there before Big Rosie could trundle his bulk around the barrier, open the wide door of the Mafia staff car and tuck his paunch under the steering wheel. If Big Rosie was angry because he thought I had gotten my wife mixed up in a murder investigation, what would he do if he thought I had poisoned Miracle as well? Apparently, my wife thought I had poisoned Miracle. Why else would she pass out?

On the road, I started to calm down. Despite all my years of putting up with learners, driving—really driving—was a balm to my soul. Maybe I should go back. Nah. Maybe I should go see

The Cobra. Nah. I had bothered her enough for one weekend. Maybe I should…crap. What was I, a man or a mouse?

So I turned the car around, headed back toward the hospital, parked behind Big Rosie who was slumped over the wheel, crushing today's rather fetching red double rose in his lapel. Big Rosie would never crush his rose. Never. Something was wrong. I sprinted inside where Double R was busy telling the clerk that he was going to kill me, Rosalie was behind him seemingly trying to calm him down by massaging his back (it was cute the way her hand seemed to make a ripple each time it went across his holster strap), Cousin Tommy was emptying the water cooler directly into his mouth by squatting in front of it and holding the lever down, and the Jadrool was literally perched on the back of a row of plastic chairs hooked together as they are with those annoying metal things that sound like nails on a blackboard when you try to pry them apart. I thought Jadrool was going to flit again, and I turned away.

I tugged on Rosalie's arm and she brushed me away. I tugged again. A roistering squeak. Then boom, clatter, shriek. The Jadrool was on the floor, struggling out of a mass of broken plastic chairs and twisted metal things. At least it broke Rosalie's attention to Double R's holster. "Rosalie," I said, literally tugging at her arm. "Big Rosie. What's with him?"

"You're worried about Big Rosie at a time like this? Your wife could have brain damage from hitting the floor like that, and you…you run off and come back and the first thing you want to know is how is Big Rosie doing? How should I know? He's right….." She looked around. "He's not here? Where's Big Rosie?"

Uh, oh. I had a feeling the Melanzane clan was about to become a large percentage of the population of Blimey-Gore

General Hospital. No, the hospital wasn't named after the mild British expletive turned backward. I'll admit, it is unusual for an NHS hospital to bear someone's name, like hospitals do in America. There, rich guys put up the dough. Here, the strapped government builds them. And they look it. But in the case of this hospital, it was a gift to the British people from two guys who came here and made a lot of money. They figured they owed us, and wanted to give back something and they liked the idea of a hospital.

The NHS relented, and Mr. Gore (who invented an artificial bull for use in the Spanish bull ring after the EU outlawed the Spanish national sport on account of cruelty to bulls, although what that has to do with England beats me, and yes, it really is his name) and Mr. Blimey (who invented nothing, but whose wealthy family's name was Blimey, I swear) donated the hospital, stem to stern.

"Big Rosie went out to his car," someone said. Not me. I didn't want them to know I knew that Big Rosie had followed me out; I didn't want them to think I was afraid of Big Rosie. So I started to move in that direction. After all, I thought, maybe it wouldn't be so bad. Big Rosie liked me now, remember? He had gotten over his initial anger after his enjoyment of Myron's road-kill story. Maybe Big Rosie wouldn't mention that I tore out of the car park as if the New York City federal prosecutor was after me. (I had to use a reference that I figured maybe Big Rosie might have thought.) Maybe the automatic seat positioning system had gone haywire and pinned the big guy. You can tell that I was feeling very warm and fuzzy about Big Rosie now.

But suddenly I was against the wall, pushed there by Rosalie's huge tatas as she ran past me toward the revolving doors, which she grabbed with a fist, and pushed her body into. She forced those flapping doors around their centre pole like an American football player trying to move one of the other behemoths off the field, all shoulder, muscle, grunts and the strain showing up the back of her calves, not bad calves considering her bulk. Maybe the gams were the last to pack on the fat. Rosie grunted harder, dug in with her formidably large canal boat feet, and extruded a few other folks like a batch of string liquorice from a machine.

(Here's another bit of useless information for you. Did you know that women on the East Coast of the US have wide feet, and the women in the Midwest have narrow ones? I'd have figured it was the other way around, what with the Midwesterners having to tromp around after cows in fields and the East Coast women mainly being commuters to office jobs. Rosalie, though, had the narrow feet of a Midwestern housewife, although she retained the disdainful, urban demeanour of Eva Longoria. And the bulk of Queen Latifah.)

Before I could adequately apologize to the three people who had run into me on their revolving door exit—two of them were still rubbing their noses which had made contact with the head in front of them, and one was looking at the booger his contact with my shirt had left—Double R was shouldering all of us out of the way so he could get to his parental couple.

I heard a couple of squeals from the clerk, and I heard the same intern walk through the door and call, "Mr. Barker." But I wasn't about to turn around. I was considering another flight. I called it off when I realized Cousin Tommy was right behind me, caressing the firearm I was sure was in his trousers pocket in an off-putting way. Either that or he was caressing something shorter in an off-putting way. But I didn't give that idea much credence.

Big Rosie was wedged under the steering wheel, his mouth opening and closing, his eyes bugging out and his hands grabbing feebly at his chest, impeded by the steering wheel and, of course, the enormous rolls of fat in his saggy upper arms.

I was right. Apparently, he had somehow slid the seat forward after he got in, and no one thought to start the car and press the electronic button to roll it back to try to extricate Big Rosie. One foot was sticking out, though, and Rosalie was down on her knees yanking backwards on that.

Double R pulled her off, and Big Rosie's shoe came, too. Nice shoe, if large. Italian leather, soft as a glove. Nice stitching. Why was I looking at a 500 quid shoe at a time like this? When else was I going to get to look at it? Usually, any foot I was trying to get a bead on was figuratively up my butt. Or wearing trainers and making magic with the accelerator in a beleaguered Car from 'L.

The intern had arrived and was standing there like he'd never seen the antics of a big, loud, Mafia Italian-American family before. I think it's called catatonia.

And then there was me. I was on my mobile phone, ringing The Cobra. A good idea to get her involved so intimately? With my extended family of gesticulating in-laws speaking what could only sound, in East Anglia, as some other form of gormless gibberish? With Miracle dead to the world inside the building. With my wife in a dead faint. Cancel…just a faint. Not a dead faint. Lord no. I loved my wife. Oy vay. I did. I loved my wife. At that moment, I realized it. Truly, fully, deeply. I loved my wife.

The family was behaving even more ludicrously than usual, although I'll grant you the circumstances were unusual, even for them. At home in Brooklyn, New York, US of A, I figured they would just have put the lot of us permanently on ice.

Still, it was clear to me that I would need The Cobra's particular talents before long, one way or another.

All that was just for starters, before the intern summoned some muscle (and some brains), turned the key in the ignition, tweaked the button and slid the seat back, rolled Big Rosie onto a lowered gurney like a whale into a transport sling, and huffed and puffed Rosie's gasping bulk into the emergency entrance and then on into a room.

It was not the calm after the storm, though, that resulted. More like the eye of a hurricane. As in the meteorological event, a good bit of the rain and wind was over, but the dead calm simply meant another, and sometimes larger, helping of tropical disaster was on its way. Not that the Italians were tropical, but they were certainly a whirlwind. I had seen them in a calm, silent mood before. Usually, someone ended up dead when the calm was over and the swirling emotions had kicked in again.

Now? Now Big Rosie was silent, or at least, if he was swearing at me, we couldn't hear it because he had been spirited away to the largest examining room so the doctors could find out what the matter was.

Rosalie was wearing out the tile in a circle around the banks of chairs. Double R was sitting, arms crossed and glowering. Cousin Tommy was cleaning his fingernails. Really. I know they always do that in gangster movies when they are discussing the next hit. But he really was cleaning his nails. Tommette was silently drinking vending machine coffee next to her husband. And the Jadrool…where WAS the Jadrool? I hadn't seen him, not really, since he turned over all those chairs. Wasn't his wife supposed to be having a baby? Why would he leave NOW?

So I went outside to see if he was still with the car. He was. He was crawling backward out of a rear passenger door, tugging at something. Oh, god. It was a black plastic bag he was tugging it…and suddenly it pulled free. It fell to the ground and clattered.

I was frozen to the spot. The Jadrool was frozen to the spot. The only person in sight who wasn't frozen to the spot—the sudden appearance of a large automatic weapon in virtually gun-free Britain can do that—was Myron, who was on his mobile, no doubt calling for backup.

TWELVE

Sympathy for the Devil

Myron hadn't called for backup. In possibly the only intelligent thing I had done all day...OK, all week...I convinced him that the Jadrool was an undercover US secret agent so the gun was perfectly OK. Myron believed me. Of course he believed me; he believed me about how to operate a motor vehicle, right? And that had worked out OK for him. Eventually. Anyway, he swallowed it and trundled his bulk back inside, all the better to aggrandize himself, no doubt, by telling the staff about his intimate acquaintance with a spy.

Whatever works, right?

Despite that small glimmer of hope that my responses to disaster were getting a bit more reliable, I was depressed. I was beginning to lose count of how many days I had lost because of the Drippers. It was almost daylight when we all left the cop house once again. Here's the rundown of those who left:

- Me
- Rosalie
- Double R
- Cousin Tommy
- Tommette
- Jadrool

In short, they released everyone they had brought in. But that didn't mean the gang that couldn't walk straight was all present and accounted for. Quite a few of our original number were still in hospital. My wife had been admitted, although she had only fainted.

"The doctors want to know why," The Cobra told me. "It isn't usual for a healthy woman of her age to just collapse."

Chloe had responded to my summons almost as if we were still married. No, that's a lie. Back then, I would have been lucky if she had responded the same month if someone had told her I was bleeding from all my orifices and my legs seemed hooked on at odd angles. So something had changed. Chloe had arrived first at the hospital and then at the cop's little outpost, after the hospital administrator told her that if she so much as returned one of us to their hallowed halls of medicine, Chloe would need a surgeon herself. Well, no, they didn't really. They DID tell her to try to control the Family if any of us cared to return to visit our sick members. And they told her what they were doing for my wife.

"They are testing to see if she's diabetic. Or pregnant," Chloe related.

I yelped. I was doing a lot of expressive stuff all of a sudden. So unlike me. So unmanly. So unBritish. Bad influence, those wildly gesticulating, globally emoting Italians.

"She's neither," I said, trusting I was right on the former, hoping I was right on the latter. What I didn't need was a half-Italian-American bambino who would doubtless be treated over its lifetime to various returnable favours from its extended transatlantic family. Which is to say, if the Godfather does something nice for you, sometime in the future, you can expect to be asked—asked?—to do something nice for him. You'll never know what or when, but you can be assured that it won't be something you would confess to your mother, your priest or the cops. Plus, I was too old. Wasn't I? My wife wasn't. I didn't exactly rob the cradle for number four, but she was considerably younger than I.

Chloe raised her eyebrows anyway. "Maybe diabetic would be better," she wisely said.

"Neither. She's fine. She just fainted because....because.... because...."

"Her husband might have croaked his boss's wife, her family was in town with all their lead-spewing hardware, an extra Goombah and Mrs. Goombah had arrived, the latter of whom was busy in the delivery suite adding souls to the ranks of garlic-lovers of the world...."

"You don't have to be so smug," I told her.

"I'm not being smug. I'm trying to get you down off the ceiling so we can actually discuss this mess."

So we went back to considering. Miracle was still in hospital and still comatose. Mrs. Jadrool had given birth but had not yet been released, but probably only because, as it turned out, she had twins and it had been a lot more difficult than the usual NHS birth. Big Rosie had been admitted. Anyone else?

"Biff."

"Your dog has been admitted to hospital?"

"No. But Holy Cow! Biff has been home alone for the past 18 hours, and I'm afraid to see what sort of condition the house is in."

But I had to. So I went home to think about this mess some more. Chloe followed in her car, while I took the L car. The journey gave me some time to think outside the range of The Cobra's TLC or criticisms, both of which she was giving me in rather large supply, considering. My wife? She was in good hands, I hoped. And besides, I thought she might be mellowing, considering how she had been with Miracle. Well, I hoped so. I had hoped so even as I had phoned The Cobra. I'm a great believer in employing people for a job who know how to do that job, and I'm not much for do-it-yourself brain surgery. I was hoping my wife would be able to extend the thaw she had experienced with Miracle to The Cobra. It wasn't too much to ask, was it? Everyone has an ex-wife or two these days, after all. It's the new normal.

And then there was Biff. He had obviously missed my wife. A lot. Because he had eaten a few of her shoes. And the pillows on the bed. Mr. Bumpy was nowhere to be seen, but he had his cat flap; I was relatively sure he would have escaped Biff's rampage and gone out to the garden. At the best of times, those two were not friends. No cute photos of cats cuddled up with dogs or sharing a bowl. I often thought of myself as the referee, to be honest.

Biff had gotten hungry, too, so he had made a meal for himself. I addition to the shoes, and pillows and NOT the cat. Or at least, Biff had figured out what the cooker was and that there was meat on top of it. So he had stood up, knocked the pot down, broken the pot—the hard-to-find, authentic totally ceramic casserole my wife used to make peposo in as well as luganica and red and green peppers—into pieces, and scarfed up the luganica. The red and green pepper slices were mashed flat on the kitchen tile, dried up on the edges, still viscous in the middle, and ground into the carpet everywhere else, making Christmassy little blobs of vibrant colour fading into beige.

At some time later, Biff apparently had to out-process the luganica, and the remains of that were facing me on the new carpeting in the living room, as well.

I went to the kitchen, got kitchen towels, clean-up spray and a plastic bag to clean up the stinking mess in the kitchen, then the hallway, and finally, the stinking mess in the living room. The Cobra went off to use the toilet.

Just as I finished putting the pile of poo into the bag and sealing it, The Cobra brushed past me and sat down as far as possible from where the dog mess had been, although now all it smelled of was chemical cleanser. She reached for a glass and the bottle of homemade hooch on the table close to her.

Luckily, my peripheral vision is exceptional; it would have to be, considering the near-disasters I have to prevent learner drivers from creating. I flew across the room, snatched the bottle from her, and sprinted to the kitchen to pour it down the sink.

She got there as I did—lithe, and springy and quick as she is—grabbed the bottle, sniffed the bottle, looked at me like I was a bug, grabbed my hand and took me and the bottle of wine back to the living room and sat down.

"Now."

"What?" What did she want?

"Well?"

She was beginning to sound a lot like Hemingway, my favourite author who could write whole scenes in one-word paragraphs and you'd end up knowing what he meant. So I spilled. Again.

"So let me get this right," Chloe said at last. "Someone put two bodies in a plastic back in an spare L car. You were questioned because a letter with your name on it was under a bag. First problem: If the bags were leaking so much they were dripping, how did this mail that so magically appeared from under them, according to Bulpitt, stay clean? Even if it had been tucked up away from them someplace, it would have smelled. No one would have wanted to pick it up, probably not even the CSI types."

"Ah." I nodded. A light bulb had gone off.

"So then you are questioned and let go. No surprise. Then you stop off to see me for the voice of reason. Then you go home and find your house is chock full of New York and New Jersey Italians. You know most of them, but there are two strangers, one about to hatch a little Sicilian potential jail bird."

I nodded. No light bulbs.

"The pregnant one goes into labour, everyone rushes to the hospital with her except you and your wife. I would have loved to see that, a veritable San Gennaro parade of Italians weaving through the streets of a quiet East Anglian city.

"Then Miracle arrives, takes one sip of the wine I am about to drink and goes comatose." Chloe picked up the glass beside her on the end table, rushed it to her mouth, and took a big slug. She kept talking. But I was sure the belladonna had been in the wine. If not there, where?

"After a lot of hurly-burly, it turns out Miracle had ingested a whopper dose of belladonna and it did her no good at all. Mrs.—what did you call her, Jadrool?—delivers herself of little Rocco Jadrool…."

"Actually, Rocco and Rockette," I said.

"Your wife faints. Big Rosie has a heart attack and is admitted and the doctors work on him, as best they can with all his fat and the coughing from the smoking. And you all—those who are conscious and not otherwise physically impaired—end up talking with the cops."

True. No more light bulbs.

"Any lose ends?" Chloe asked. "Anyone or anything missing?"

I told her there was still no news on who body number two might be, I had no idea where the rest of the Melanzane/Jadrool contingent was, I hoped my wife was OK, I hoped Miracle would be OK, I didn't care all that much about Big Rosie despite his slight thawing toward me, didn't know about Myron, didn't know or care about Bulpitt or Ignatz or much of anything else at that moment except food, sleep, and a call to the hospital to see about my wife.

"So."

***

When I awoke—Chloe had moved my legs up onto the sofa and covered me with a coat—Chloe was just about finished with the bottle of poisoned wine.

"I thought I would just drink myself silly while you napped," she said. "I covered you with your coat." She wasn't silly, though. The woman had the capacity of an Irish dockworker. Or maybe the fact that she had eaten most of the remaining ciabatta, which was not to Biff's taste—along with some lovely Asiago cheese I had brought home several days ago—kept her sober.

"It's not my coat."

"No? Whose?"

"I don't know," I said groggily. "Jadrool's? Maybe Big Rosie's. Yeah, it has to be Big Rosie's; it covered me like a tent."

I began to squeeze the coat. At least I couldn't feel a gun anywhere in it. But I did feel something. I squeezed it, felt around the pockets. It seemed to be in the lining. It was like a cylinder of some sort.

Chloe got the scissors out of the kitchen drawer—how did she know where to find them? Right, a woman thing. Anyway, although I was sure I was taking my life in my hands, we slit Big Rosie's coat open and out popped a plastic cylinder. We opened that, and out popped all sorts of cash. Well, not all sorts. Just a huge amount of American cash. Nice that their folding money is so narrow; you can get a lot more of it into a small tube than you could pounds sterling.

"So, Big Rosie carries a lot of cash. What else is new?" I said.

Chloe just considered. "What does he do, for a living, I mean?"

I didn't know, not then. And I didn't feel right about telling my ex-wife that my current wife's pseudo-daddy was a Mafia hit man, because, frankly, I really didn't know if he was. I don't like to cast aspersions on anyone, but least of all on huge, powerfully built older men with Italian surnames, homes in New Jersey, USA, and lots of guns that he can apparently bring into England. So we began pawing around in the rest of Rosie's overcoat and found a few cryptic messages about horses. "So he plays the ponies," I said. "But why hide it?"

"We have a lot of holes to fill in here before we will know what's going on," Chloe said. "First, who zapped Miracle, when and why? It wasn't the wine; I proved that, but I knew that anyway."

Why did she know that? Why had she even thought about it? It was pretty low on my lifetime thoughts priorities list, really. I was more interested in how my wife—my current wife—was doing.

"Second, who is the second dripper? We won't know until the cops know…unless we find out first some other way than forensics. Who are the Jadrools? Why were they in your house? And most importantly, how did Big Rosie and friends get here that fast? You can't get through airport security in the US that fast, never mind book a ticket, get through security even if you elect the full-body irradiation instead of the hand job, fly across an ocean and stink up someone's house. Holy Crimean War, what the hell is that smell?"

I could at least answer Chloe's last question. It was the remainder of the Biff stink from the Circle of Shame still evident on the carpet even after my earlier ministrations, and rising like incense since the central heating in the house had switched on. I don't deal very well with the Circle of Shame. Usually my wife does the cleanup as I tend to gag. So doubtless, I had missed some particles of Eau de Crapeau.

And the other part of the fug was a combination of Ronson-lighter fluid perfume added to the atmosphere by the warm, heaving chests of three Mafia molls who had dented the sofa for a few hours, plus Rosalie's mama-bear scent mixing with cooking smells from the kitchen, and the molecular traces of Big Rosie's cigar that had fled the garden to take up more comfortable residence inside, where they wouldn't be blown away and could hang around creating a proper setting for remembering our guests for a long time to come.

How did she know it wasn't the wine that got Chloe? I asked.

"Simples," she said, and clicked like a TV advert meerkat. "It was belladonna."

"Belladonna? How could you know that?" I felt like an idiot right after I asked. She was a private detective; she earned her money by knowing things like that. Did I really care how she knew it? No. I just wanted my life back. So I said so.

"I just want my life back." I paused, but she didn't offer anything. "So what do we do now?" I asked, warming to the task of figuring out some of this, any of this.

Chloe looked daggers at me. "You know, that sounds a lot like what Tony Hayward said that pissed off the Americans big time."

"What?"

"He was referring to the BP oil spill in the Gulf of Mexico. He said he wanted the spill to stop, too. He said, 'I would like my life back'." The Americans pointed out that eleven men had lost their lives, and millions of animals as well. Callous, to say the least, especially since we Brits claim to have higher sensibilities than that."

"Shit."

"Exactly. However, I'm wondering if Hayward's gormless attitude can't help us solve this mess," Chloe said. "Someone here has started a shit fest that is stinking up a lot of lives—yours, Miracle's, your wife's, mine. And somehow, Big Rosie and Bulpitt—talking about strange bedfellows—are involved."

I couldn't argue with that. But how? And what next?

As it happened, I didn't have to wonder too long about what was next, because there was a knock at the door, or at least, I think that's what caused Biff to go all wild and bark and jump up in front of the door. Before I could answer it, the door opened. Biff banged it closed. It opened again. Biff banged it again. Chloe looked at me. I looked at her, and raised my eyebrows. I had not heard a car pull up. Maybe it was someone selling something. We had a gypsy woman by not long ago wanting to sell something. I don't know what. I don't even believe gypsies are gypsies, or not gypsies, but you know what I mean. Who knows what's the truth? So we don't open the door, usually, and if we do, we bang it shut again as soon as possible.

And then I heard Andy Devine. "Rosalie," I said, hauling Biff away from the door.

"I'm starving. Big Rosie is in intensive care. Whatshername is still there with the twin boys...."

"Oy."

"I didn't know you knew Yiddish," Rosalie said. "Anyway, Double R and his wife are sleeping at our hotel. So's Tommy and his wife. And your wife…."

"What?"

"Your wife is fine, but they want to keep her a day or so because she got quite a knock on the head when she fell. You gonna go see her, or what? And I'm hungry. Who's this?"

"This is Chloe, my ex-wife," I said. "She's a detective."

"I gotta go."

"I thought you were hungry."

Rosalie was rising, not an inconsiderable process considering her bulk. Chloe pushed her back down. "No, you need to eat," Chloe told her, acting like a real human being, which of course I didn't expect from her. Mainly because I was obtuse; hadn't she already helped me out? Hadn't she come to my house of her own volition to help me out some more? Hadn't she covered me with a blanket and let me sleep for a couple of hours? Wasn't I getting a big maudlin? When you've got a mind as active as mine, you've got to police (no, bad word choice)…that is, monitor your choice of words, even in self-talk, all the time.

"Shelf, go get Rosalie something to eat," Chloe said, and I did as bidden. I went to the kitchen, opened the fridge and saw what I thought I would see. Nothing. So I went to the pantry, opened the door, and saw what I thought I would see. Dog food and cat food. So I picked up my car keys and headed out to Spar, leaving Chloe and Rosalie alone in the living room, except for Mr. Bumpy who had crawled into Chloe's meagre lap; why didn't he pick Rosalie's lap? It's softer. Biff was with me.

THIRTEEN

Heartbreak Hotel

It all seemed like a bad dream. How could I wake up one morning in East Anglia, doing as I had been doing for some time—trying to get through a day of driver wannabes of various levels of skill and various degrees of mental health—and the next in Brooklyn, NY, US of A, attending a Mafia funeral?

And yet, it had happened, but not until after a whole lot of other stuff had happened as well. Here's how it went down, as they say in the mob (I'm getting comfortable with this stuff now.)

I got back from Spar with some kind of packaged sandwich and a bag of crisps—chips to Americans; chips to Brits are French Fries, but we have abhorred the French a lot longer than the Yanks have. The Yanks just began really hating the French when they wouldn't join Baby Bush in his Iraqi escapades. Chips they have been to Brits from time immemorial, and chips they shall remain. Can you imagine a Fish and Fries shop? Well, yes, actually. But I digress. Let's leave it at crisps, and move on.

The phone rang and I answered it and that's the next time I really wanted either to die or kill someone. It was my wife. On the phone, not in my crosshairs.

"Shelf, please come and get me now. They want to keep me, but I want to go home. I'm not angry; I know you would have come except you needed some sleep and Biff probably needed walking...."

In an instant, after the paralysing fear that had gripped me when I first heard her voice on the phone and wondered what hell she would put me through for leaving her in my craven cowardice, I was suddenly so in love with my Italian angel I could cry. Even more in love than earlier. I told her I'd come right away, as soon as I took care of Rosalie. You really shouldn't say "take care of" to a Mafia family, as it has more than one meaning. But just to prove she wasn't really Mafia, my wife didn't even flinch. She just blew me a kiss over the phone. My hard heart melted some more. And then I saw Chloe. She was staring at me like as if I was a brand new Biff Spot of Shame, all smelly and viscous. Or so I thought.

"It's all right, Shelf," she said. "I'm not in love with you anymore, and you're not in love with me, so it's cool. I'm happy you finally found out what a nice person your current wife is. You just let your previous disastrous unions colour your perceptions."

"Oh, shut up," I said, not really meaning it. So she wasn't looking at me as if I were something foul; she was trying to figure out what she was seeing. I could have blushed, but men don't.

"Hey. Ovah here. Helloooo…." Rosalie sang out. "Where's my food? In your hot mitts while I'm starving. Junk, you got me. Junk. No tomatoes (she said toMAYtoes), no nuthin'. Well, whatever. I gotta eat for Big Rosie's sake." She began to chow down right where she was, within sniffing distance of Biff's ex-deposit, among the new dirty wine glasses, on top of Big Rosie's coat that had lain for quite some time where it landed where I had flung it after Chloe and I had ransacked it.

The coat! Holy mother of god, I thought. What about the money? I looked at Chloe. She shook her head. We let Rosalie continue to eat; we would get back to the coat later.

Anyway, I had to leave to go get my wife. And then the phone rang again.

I thought it was my wife—maybe she wanted a change of clothes or something. But it was the hospital, looking for Mrs. Melanzane. I put Rosalie on. She listened for a few minutes, and slumped against the wall. She got pale. Really pale. Not easy for the swarthy types. Chloe ran to her side, as women do. I stood there with my bare face hanging out, as men do. Mr. Bumpy stalked into the hallway headed toward one or another comfy bed, not caring what was happening in the odd world of humans, as cats do. Biff sat and drooled, as dogs do, with a fairly stupid expression on his face, I thought.

The good news was that Rosalie did not faint. We had had enough, I think, of fainting and such things for one weekend. Week. Whatever. It was bad news, and it was bad even though he was a Mafia don, because any death is sad—Big Rosie had died.

There was no question about what would happen next. I would take Rosalie to the hospital; there were forms to fill out, arrangements to make. I would fetch my wife. I would be strong. I would be a man. And I would have Chloe to help me, because she volunteered; because I am probably really only half a man, I accepted.

The next couple of days passed in that sort of blur that always happens when someone close to you dies. Big Rosie wasn't close, exactly, but he had developed, belatedly, a grudging respect for me, and I appreciated that. And, since he was the closest thing my wife had to a father, I was sorry for my wife's sake. As for my wife, she was grieving quite a bit. And Rosalie?

Well, you have not heard grief until you have heard it from an Italian matriarch of some years. You've heard of banshees wailing? Not enough. You've heard the terror of a million souls blown to smithereens by the Death Star in Star Wars? Not enough. The grief wail of at least one Italian-American matriarch was enough to peel the shellac off a Georgian highboy. And it went on for the length of a Pavarotti high note. This was grief so intense in its expression that I didn't even want to imagine the effect of it on every cell in Rosalie's body; it was making my own sorry innards quake with misery.

The fact that Rosalie had spent her life waiting on Big Rosie, although they could well have afforded servants, was not relevant. The fact that her nice clothes, good jewellery, big house, luxury cars and trips to Miami probably resulted from her husband whacking some jerk? Also not relevant.

The only thing that was relevant was grief and the wailing that resolved into crying, and at length, into eating. By god, the woman could pack it in. I always heard you didn't eat when you were that grief-stricken. And there is no doubt in my mind she was grief-stricken. But we almost had the Waitrose delivery van on a scheduled run between their local largest emporium and our front door. It wasn't like in Brooklyn, where neighbours would be coming through with lasagnes and rum cakes and grappa and coffee that would melt stolen car parts and noshing and condolencing. It was just us. Just Rosalie Melanzane, my wife, me, Mr. and Mrs. Double R Melanzane, Cousin and Mrs. Cousin Tommy Melanzane and Mr. Jadrool; Mrs. Jadrool had been sent home with the two little purple-looking twins with blue-black sunken eye sockets and spindly cooked-Turkey-looking legs and needed to spend time with them, or so the story went.

And Chloe showed up, too, as often as she could get away from the cheating-husband-stalking job she was on. Those paid the bills; more interesting stuff—such as finding maladjusted middle-aged women who stuffed helpless kittens into trash bins—didn't pay well, but it made her feel good. Frankly, to my mind, apprehending Bin Woman was a better service to mankind that putting the noose around the neck of a husband whose attentions has strayed, and should have been worth more, but what did I know? And who would pay her excessively for that? The maladjusted crone? The cops? The kitten's owner? Well, maybe them. But it wasn't close to what a wronged wife would pay to see her husband forever in bondage to the UK courts, which are rather vicious about turning over large amounts of an ex-husband's income to a lazy ex-wife. I should know.

NO, not Chloe. One of the others. Not the one who took off for Burma—Myanmar? whatever—and has been shacked up with some swami avoiding the secret police, last I heard. That one is not within the confines of the UK's watchful waiters who snag errant fathers and alimony avoiders, but it's not worth it. I pay up. Did I mention the long hours I work? I wonder when that guru is going to teach her the wisdom of living frugally, like a sadhvi for example, and writing to the British courts that she no longer wishes to receive payments from her ex-husband.

I should explain, as not everyone will have spent time learning all there is to know about eastern religions, the better to conduct classes in yoga and meditation. Sadvhi are female sadhus. Sadhus are holy men of India and Nepal who have left behind all material and sexual attachments, living rough wherever they can find shelter—caves, forests, temples.

***

In due course, the arrangements were made. Big Rosie's mortal remains would be transported to New York's John F. Kennedy Airport, accompanied on that sad journey by all those named above, except the Jadrools. (I knew I would have to find out their real name sooner or later, but Jadrool was fine for the time being.) Naturally, my wife was among those meant to go, as was I. Not naturally, The Cobra also booked a ticket, at the insistence of my wife.

FOURTEEN

For What It's Worth

There is nothing like a Roman Catholic funeral in that most Italian of the Italian neighbourhoods in Brooklyn, New York —Carroll Gardens—to get one thinking about the possible connections among the family of man. The morning of Big Rosie's funeral, it was bright, that kind of bright you only get with a winter sun sneaking between buildings, bouncing off them, lighting up the trees growing out of door-sized patches of grass cut through the pavement (Yanks call it sidewalk) and reflecting down again. There are all sorts of colours in that sun; yellow, white, grey from the buildings, a reddish glow from brickwork, blue and green.

The kaleidoscope doesn't end there, though. You've got to include the bazaar of humanity clogging Brooklyn streets from the minute the first Nana toddles out in her black silk dress to the greengrocers at 9 a.m. until Mama stands on the stoop at dusk calling Angelo to come home. I didn't know what a stoop was until I landed in New York. Soon, I figured out it was one of two things, depending on how it was spelled…which you can't tell by hearing it, but I asked.

A stupe is a dopey person—that is, stupid—as in, "Get offa my new car, ya stupe. I don' wan' it scratched up."

A stoop is what New Yorkers call a flight of six or so steps leading up to the front door. Not surprisingly, it is a Dutch word since the Dutch owned New York before we Brits did and before the colonists liberated it, as they might say in the New World. So here it is in a sentence: "Go wait for me on the stoop at the Schitt house. I'll be right along. They won't mind." OK, three sentences. But I've been trying to find a use for Schitt house ever since I thought of it, mulling all that Dutch stuff in my overworked brain. But maybe Schitt is German. Who cares? It's Germanic, and that's enough for me. No, research was not my strong suit at the University of Ye Gods and Little Fishes.

While attempting to find out if my made-up name for a Brooklyn family that might own a stoop was real, I came across an Americanism that's hard to beat: You don't know Jack Schitt, to denote someone who is talking through his hat. Naturally, in this era of the internet, someone made up a family tree for Jack Schitt. It goes like this:

> Jack Schitt is the only son of O. Schitt and Awe Schitt. O. Schitt, the fertilizer magnate, married Awe Schitt, who later ran the Kneedeep Inn-Schitt. Jack Schitt eventually married Noe Schitt, and together they produced six children. Holy Schitt, their first child, passed on shortly after birth. Next came twin sons, Deep Schitt and Dip Schitt and then two daughters, Fulla Schitt and Giva Schitt. Their final child, another son, named Bull Schitt. In the meantime, Deep Schitt married Dumb Schitt, a high school dropout. Dip Schitt married Lotta Schitt and they have a son, Chicken Schitt. Fulla Schitt and Giva Schitt married the Happens Brothers. The Schitt-Happens children are Dawg Schitt, Bird Schitt and Horace Schitt. Bull Schitt just married a spicy number, Pisa Schitt and they are expecting the arrival of Baby Schitt.

***

My wife and I and Chloe had taken rooms in a hotel on the Brooklyn waterfront, not the old waterfront with the dockyard, the new one with the pleasure boats all lined up on floating docks. The area was called Marine Park, and it seemed to cater to Polish immigrants, not Italian. Still, it was only a short cab ride to Carroll Gardens, and my wife seemed to prefer being a little distance from the collected Melanzanes, Boccigalupis, Bellavitas, Dellabrasinos, etc. Maybe she was ashamed of her white-bread spouse.

Anyway, it was a nice taxi ride to the church. First you get on the Shore Parkway/Belt Parkway, then Ocean Parkway, then Prospect Parkway, then the Gowanus Expressway. Only one of them is aptly named, the Gowanus Expressway. The Gowanus Canal, over which it passes, would probably be improved by a few dead cows floating down it, Ganges-like. As for the rest, there is nothing park like about them, except if you include the fact that some mutant trees have been planted down the central reservations in places. In other places, the central reservations sport park benches, on which welfare recipients are parked all day doing nothing.

Then you get to Carroll Gardens, where everyone is busy and everything is spic and span. Even the little shrines to the Virgin in front of the houses are sparkling with whitewash and tender, loving care. They are wiped of soot frequently, and any pigeon schitt that lands on them is soaped away immediately by the lady of the house, wearing her flower-sprigged cotton housecoat and over-at-the-heel, not-for-the-street canal boats. No makeup will have been applied this early, and rollers might still sprout from under a filmy scarf.

The church where we ended up was quaintly named the Church of Sts. Martha, Elizabeth, Tiffany, Brittany and All the Holy Mothers. Where the church was placed, it sort of triangulated the once-and-future swell neighbourhood of

Brooklyn Heights were the WASPs lived (white Anglo-Saxon Protestants, as opposed to Sicilians), the Brooklyn Navy Yard (docks) and Red Hook (even rougher docks.)

Once we got there, the air was thick with incense and the wails of Rosalie and all the women in her family and all of her female friends. My wife was family. And just when I was getting to be really fond of her, and then the wailing…I'm kidding. She did sniffle a bit, but was actually much more composed than most of the dolls and the goombahs filling the church.

The solemn-faced ushers led us to the family pews at the front of the church. Chloe was included in his sweeping gesture of welcome and repose, but chose to hang back for, I supposed, a better view of the panorama, and possibly to see what information she could glean. That was, after all, why she had come.

"You're bringing your ex-wife to my father's funeral?" Double R had said earlier, when we had to pass him on the broad front steps. It wasn't menacing. More like he didn't understand how anyone could be such a moron.

"It's all right," my wife told him. "Chloe is my best friend in all the world and she can help me through this. I don't want to burden Shelf with all my grief."

Double R swallowed it, but then, he didn't have much choice. He shrugged those huge shoulders, let his pointy head slide back down on his rump roast neck and settle above the metallic knot of his silver, purple and black funeral tie.

Despite the aspersions my wife cast on my ability to help her through her grief, I seemed to have found my manhood sometime between discovering my wife's suddenly forgiving nature and grasping the certain knowledge that one of my biggest long-standing problems—Big Rosie—had been neutralized. Or in other words, croaked. Better still, his demise was from natural causes, the doctors said, so Double R had no reason to hate me (whew!), and also, none of us had to fear the church being riddled with bullets from a rival "family." How often does that happen, I wondered, that a Mafia don dies of natural causes? Still, any death in the upper echelons could set off a sort of bullet-enhanced bidding war for territory, I had been told. Nah. I wouldn't worry about that now.

Besides, my rift with Big Rosie had been healed. A pat on the back by Big Rosie at the hospital after Myron's story was almost enough to overcome years of Sicilian high disdain (his) for Anglo-Saxon timidity (mine). The lord moves in mysterious ways his wonders to perform.

Plus, I had managed to seek out my ex-wife for her valuable skills while keeping my current wife happy. No, ecstatic. She was ecstatic. And no, it's not what you think. She was simply glad that I had accompanied her on the journey, had introduced her to The Cobra (who can understand the ways of women?) and was treating her as if I really loved her, at last. Still, if God had any more wonders available, I was praying they would come my way when we got back to England because the constabulary had informed me that they would like another wee tête-à-tête when I returned.

With that in the back of my mind, I was determined to enjoy this spectacle of Latin grief as much as possible.

FIFTEEN

Brooklyn Roads

The aforementioned spectacle did not disappoint.

I hate to admit it, but I was developing a grudging respect for my wife's family during the days crying and nights of drinking in Carroll Gardens, Brooklyn, New York. Unlike in England, where stiffs—jeez, I'm using mob speak again—where decedents are not buried until a couple of weeks after death, in the United States, it's more like three days. Sometimes less. For Big Rosie Melanzane, it was a full week. Why? Because we all had to arrange and accomplish the journey from the Old Country. And because the church—the aforementioned Sts. Martha, Elizabeth, Tiffany, Brittany and All the Holy Mothers—had some experience with conducting Mafia funerals. They knew they would see a steady stream of mourners from right after eight o'clock mass until the doors were locked at 6 p.m. for a lot longer than two days, followed by a morning mass and interment.

I'm not sure all the traipsing into the church had much to do with praying for the repose of the soul of the goombah known as Big Rosie in this instance. It might have had something to do with the bleeding statue. I had heard that such things happened in the New World, but it didn't occur to me that they might occur in an Italian community, at an Italian-American Roman Catholic Church and especially it didn't occur to me that such a thing would happen during the funeral week of Big Rosie. In fact, the bleeding had begun the first day of the viewing of Big Rosie's former husk. At least it wasn't on a main statue, not on Martha,

Elizabeth, Tiffany or Brittany. All the Holy Mothers? One was meant to infer them, as there was no platoon of female saints beyond the aforementioned.

The bleeding got started on the image of St. Christopher, patron saint of motorists. I know why the bleeding got started there. It was because of me. Really. It turns out that it was OK for the church to have the statue, as Chris was still officially a saint to the Romans. But Pope Paul VI had taken his feast day off the official calendar, so the statue was really of no use to the church. No reason to wreath it in flowers and so on. In fact, Paul VI was probably more meaningful to me, a lapsed Church of England member, because he was the first pope to receive and recognize officially the Archbishop of Canterbury. To some, the Archbishop is a nobody, the Queen (or King, as the case may be) being the official head of the Church of England, despite not being legal to celebrate the sacraments on account of not being ordained, just crowned. Crowned trumps ordained…except when it doesn't. But Paul VI had lots of time to monkey with church stuff; his successor, John Paul I had no time even to hear the joke about the Schitts, never mind baptize them. He lasted only 33 days until someone croaked him. Oh? You say. Has that been proven? Nah, but my mind is on violent death at the moment, and coupling my recent experiences with the bleeding statue, well, it has all been too much for me, and I might almost be able to forget that Pope John Paul I's sudden death has never been satisfactorily explained. I sort of wonder how the Mackerel Snappers can live with that. After all, the sudden demise of Thomas á Becket, medieval Archbishop of Canterbury, has been explained admirably, even in films. Richard Burton played the saint and Peter O'Toole played King Henry II, who ordered the murder. Only one of those actors could possibly have been typecast.

Anyway, it would seem there was more than one reason for the statue of St. Christopher to start bleeding when I entered the church. But it wasn't blood. I turned out that, as is usually the case, a water leak was simply dripping onto the Saint and causing the terracotta under the cheap paint to show through. The newspapers didn't even arrive for a photo shoot before the maintenance man figured it out, although doubtless several of the old women had phoned in the tip. Still, it did give people something else to talk about when they stopped by the funeral home, or funeral parlour as it was more often called by the locals.

There, we sat around on silk-covered sofas with gilded legs, put on our sad faces, and murmured thanks for coming to a parade of the blessed and the damned, as they trotted along from the church after lighting candles, dropping some money in the poor box, and saying a rosary over Rosie's soul that would have warmed the cockles of the heart of any medieval abbot in the world.

There were the old grandmothers, not so many in the storied black silk dress and cheek-tugging bun these days, usually in a beige linen-look polyester pantsuit and apricot-colour hair from the House de Beauté. I never saw wrinkles like that, though, on living women. You might think you could barely see the wrinkles for the glimmering fruit-coloured hair, but the upper lips were more wrinkles than not, and all in a sort of avocado-pit hue, like the rest of the face. Except the lips. The lips were uniformly some version of *Some Like It Hot* red, weeping into the lines around the lips. Naturally. I asked my wife how they got so many wrinkles, considering Italian skin is not paper-thin like English skin . "They smoke," she said. "All of them. For years. Like chimneys. You would too if you never knew whether your husband was going to be the whacker or the whackee.

"And before you ask, no they were not all Mafia wives. Of course not. Some were married to longshoremen, or bricklayers. Honourable honest jobs. But if you got in trouble, especially in the old days, you asked the capo for help. He helped you. Then you owed him. And your wife worried. Bingo."

AHA! So. It really was like the old movies. I thought I was being dramatic, worrying earlier about what I would owe the don if I ever had a child with my wife and Big Rosie ever helped us out. *What the hell was I doing here?*

Enjoying myself, if the truth be known. The grandmothers all had daughters and grand-daughters and great-grand-daughters. And frankly, until the smoking and worrying took its toll, these were some beautiful women. Voluptuous, even though I really thought their endowments were not quite as grand as what my old best friend used to call "Big Celtic titties" to be found on the Anglo-Celtic-Saxon tribe. Still, there were good hips, enough tushie to grab onto, and often long slender legs. Nice hair. Nice eyes. Nice lips. Until age kicked in, at least. Any man worth his salt would enjoy looking. If I were anyone else, I might have stood by the casket—open, naturally—and watched as they knelt down to say a prayer over Big Rosie's chemical-filled self. I bet it was a treat.

Maybe that's what Cousin Tommy's eleven-year-old son was up to. He was very solicitous of the ladies, helping them down to the kneeler where Big Rosie lay in his solid mahogany "Chicago overcoat" and back up again. The kid was good, though. He never once smiled. Of course, the Italians have the grief thing whacked, what with having so many funerals, especially during turf wars, and enjoying them so much. (Please excuse my bad choice of words. I meant to say that they have it down pat.)

Another thing about it all was amazing. I never had never seen an open casket before. It isn't done in England. I was surprised they did it for members of The Organization, considering many of them died from lead poisoning and some from the Harlem sunrise. Oh, sorry; being shot or being stabbed. I wasn't too stupid to pick up on the conversations I overheard in the toilets, usually about some mark or palooka that got in the way of business. I didn't go to the toilets much; it didn't take a genius to figure out they wouldn't like it if their exploits were known outside of the family, The Family, or the church. I didn't get all the slang anyway. For example, I'm still confused about shylock and shyster; one means lawyer, the other means loan shark. Either way, the Melanzanes and friends knew lots of each. And all of them seemed to school about the funeral parlour from one end of the day to the other.

Each day, at six, we would all troop out to dinner. The entire gang. Me, my wife, Rosalie, the Cousin Tommy family, Double R and wife, some of the assorted Melanzane offspring, Chloe. We ate at one of three restaurants, Ristorante Marco Polo, Vinny's, or Junior's.

Marco Polo was the upscale venue. All sorts of fake Italian sandstone on the façade, and inside, more adventurous sorts of Northern Italian dishes. Sicily, where the family came from, is not so adventurous about its food. But Double R and family had developed a taste for nouveau Italian food, the stuff Lidia Bastianich, TV chef, taught so well. For instance, I had an appetizer of goat's cheese, caramelised onions, polenta and fig balsamic vinegar. I could have had the same thing in any number of Italian restaurants in London. But somehow, having it in

Carroll Gardens, home of the first Roman Catholic church serving an Italian parish in storied Brooklyn, New York, made it that much more exciting. That, and the fact that the owner would appear, inquire after our condition, send a little something 'for the table'—some recently made buffalo mozzarella, roasted red peppers—and was generally a nice guy.

I couldn't say, actually, that my wife's family was anything but nice guys, even if they were wise guys. You had to wonder; how did they fit the whacking stuff in there?

But Rosalie had to have her "gravy," or tomato sauce aplenty. So we went to Vinny's, too, where there were huge plates full of great pasta and gravy. I was getting fat. But I had developed a taste for cannoli that I didn't think was going to leave me alone after I got home. I hoped I could find it in East Anglia, or even London. For cannoli, I would drive. Kill? Nah. Well, maybe.

For a change, we went to Junior's. Junior's was not Italian. It was founded in 1950 by a Jewish guy, Harry Rosen, but it was a New York institution. Mainly, Junior's was cheesecake. It was *NEW YORK* cheesecake. Creamy and light? No. Heavy, dense, full of cheese with very little cake. A bottom crust. That's all. It came in flavours—pumpkin swirl, chocolate swirl, topped with cherries. As I said, I was getting fat. The hamburgers were a good prelude to the cheesecake.

We had a good time over dinner. Even Rosalie perked up, joined in the inevitable argument. The main one was about Big Rosie's overcoat.

"Where is Big Rosie's overcoat?" she tossed out one evening. She had tossed it out before, always tearfully. This time, she meant business.

"Right. Where is it?" Double R said, looking at me.

Cousin Tommy joined in. Each time, I raised my eyebrows and shrugged. The Cobra didn't shrink from it; she stared them down. Was that wise?

After several nights of minutely parsing where Big Rosie's coat might have ended up—the rented car? The hospital?—they finally decided the Jadrool might have taken it, cheap little bastard that he was (they said; I wouldn't know), and after the funeral, Double R would go back to England and get the coat or die trying. That is, Jadrool would die, to get it straight. Oy.

Finally, the morning of the funeral mass and interment arrived. Bright and early, we dressed in our blackest blacks, having all been shopping at Macy's during the week to augment our bereavement togs. Not wanting to appear underdressed—this was a mob funeral, remember—we had also visited a jewellery store. There, the ladies obtained a couple of diamond tennis bracelets, as well as some other ice; a couple of rings, some earrings, a lariat necklace for each of them. Good thing my wife's ex had left her loaded.

SIXTEEN

We Gotta Get Out of This Place

We wouldn't get the limo treatment until after the funeral mass, so we all had to arrive by our own means. My wife and Chloe and I had called a car service, something like a taxi only you can book them ahead, and usually the cars are clean. And besides, with all that ice dripping from the ladies, we didn't think flashing it around on the subway, which originated in Red Hook before entering Carroll Gardens, was a good idea. Red Hook is being gentrified, but it spent a few decades as the armpit of south Brooklyn, and we didn't want to take a chance that it was still a vermin-ridden, gang-sprouting haven for human detritus, much as its beloved Gowanus Canal was for detritus of other kinds, from old cars and PCB effluent, to croaked jadrools. But that's for later.

***

When we drove up to the church, there was a gaggle of people on the pavement. No, correction, a gaggle of men. All of them beefy. All of them wearing black suits. Shiny black suits. With fur-trimmed overcoats over their arms. Did I mention the season? Doesn't matter. A made man will almost always have a fur-trimmed overcoat somewhere in the vicinity.

To the mob, a "made man" is one who has killed. Not too different from the youth gangs in America, except for one thing. The mob kills only its own wayward sons; the youth gangs kill at random. Do I admire the mob for their scruples? Let's put it this way: At least it is logical and, to them, meaningful. It keeps members in line, while minimizing the chances that the cops will expend much effort on bringing the killers to justice. The youth gang's way is illogical. It doesn't keep members in line for the simple reason that the cops are looking for the killer since innocent people have been murdered, not just other criminals about whom the cops couldn't care less. Additionally, there is no expectation to keep the gang's secrets, like the *omerta* code of silence in the mob; youth gang members squeal on each other in ways that would make any self-respecting Mafia don turn in his grave. Usually, the youth gang members sing to save their sorry hides. If a made man sang, his sorry tush might be saved from federal prosecution, but he'd be fertilizer in some row-house back garden—or maybe under the sports complex known as The Meadowlands—before long.

Two of the beefy guys were Double R and Cousin Tommy. I counted, altogether, five wise guys. Not including the several funeral director types in their dark gray morning suits. I don't think they were wise guys. Made men? Nah. They didn't croak people; they just planted them.

As we got out of the car, Double R beckoned. Me?

Me. I told the ladies to go inside and I'd join them. My wife rolled her eyes; she knew.

When I joined the palaver, Double R told me he hoped I was stronger than I looked because Big Rosie was pretty heavy even with the life gone out of him. I had never been a pall bearer; in England, it's all done by the funeral director's staff, with the family just following behind. In New York, we were expected to heft the stiff, his clothing (I supposed), the mahogany box all duded up with brass and putti, and a blanket of roses fit for the winner at Ascot's Opening Day.

Of course it was roses. It had to be for Big Rosie Melanzane, about whom both Chloe and I hoped we would learn more during the priest's eulogy. For Chloe, it was professional curiosity. For me…well, it would be nice to learn a little bit more about the big man who had hated me and then respected me because one of my students was a jerk. Go figure. Why Myron's tale of killing donkeys in Cornwall should have turned the page for me, I'll never know. Still, the fact that Big Rosie had come to a grudging appreciation of me as his favorite niece's husband at least enabled me to get a bit teary eyed over his death.

I turned with the other family members after we set the mahogany box in the center of the aisle in front of the altar steps. We didn't really carry it. It was on a dead-guy gurney, so we just had to grasp the handles and push it up the aisle. We didn't even have to carry it inside from the hearse; the gurney thing had springs and with the help of two funeral directors, we got it up the front steps with very little grunting and groaning. Pushing it down the center aisle so it could be sprinkled with holy water by the priest and tromped past by the rest of us was a doddle.

We pallbearers didn't get any help from the Navy honour guard that was stationed near the doors. I couldn't believe it. Not that they didn't help; that they were there at all. But Big Rosie had served in the Navy. He always wore a little lapel pin of the Stars and Stripes, so I guessed he was proud of his country, too. Who wouldn't be, a country that had mobsters entertaining in the White House…or at least, everyone figured Dean Martin and his Rat Pack for mobsters. One of them, Peter Lawford, was married to a Kennedy—JFK's sister Patricia—for crying out loud. I hate to admit it, but Peter Lawford was British, a good looking guy as are we all, if a little low on the body hair bell curve, as we all are. Lawford became a Yank just in time to help with Jack Kennedy's campaign for president. Just goes to show there's as much scum in high places as low ones. Anyway, isn't America the land of equality?

I went and sat down next to my wife, who was next to Chloe, who was next to Mrs. Cousin Tommy in the last row of family. I looked around. We looked like a bunch of birds with black feathers and very odd plumage. The hair colors of the men? Boring, disproving the idea that the male of the species is more resplendent than the female. Black hair, mainly, if any. There were a few with slick skulls. Then the black suits. From the back, blackbirds. From the front? Blackbirds with bling. I wish I had a penny for every ounce of gold on mens' fingers in that church. And the tie clasps. And lapel pins, usually some form of American flag, but red, white and blue stones set into gold. I hadn't realized how much the mob loved their ice…uh…diamonds.

The women were another story. Very colourful. They were all wearing hats, but peeking out was every shade of hair known to man and some not yet identified…but no purple or green, I was happy to note. All "natural" colors, with a particular emphasis on what I'm going to call Sopranos Strawberry Blonde. And of course the apricot of the old dolls. And a very small smattering of the dark, dark, dark chestnut hair found naturally among Italians, at least in Italy. All that stuff about haplogroups, and so on. In our row, anchored on the far side by some second cousins 19 times removed, all with varying shades of auburn hair, there was Chloe, a natural blonde (ahem.) Then my wife, who had taken liberties with her natural dark chestnut until it had a sort of ethereal glow, from skillful and doubtless expensive and time-consuming highlighting, I think. Then me. My head of fine ginger-colored hair, with its receding hairline and what many thought its excessive length, nonetheless stood up like a beacon. A sort of human dandelion thistle. It must have looked a treat next to the deep red roses on Big Rosie's bier when I had hefted His Largeness onto my scrawny shoulder, in concert with—if a little staggery—the beefy bearers. Next to the Melanzanes, I looked like an albino stork. Fortunately, I was merely a ginger, a unique and wonderful creature making up part of only 1 to 2 percent of the entire population of the globe. I looked a bit like Art Garfunkel, only not so blond. I was a ginger person, and in the UK, that is—as the Yanks would say—nothing to write home about. So I admit it. I don't look like Matthew Modine in *Married to the Mob*. I look like Art Garfunkel, and I hoped not the way he looked in *Catch-22*, at the end. Dead. Cut in half in an airplane mishap. Spouting blood and guts. The Melanzanes didn't have airplanes—did they?—but they were quite experienced at blood and guts.

As the priest intoned whatever it is they intone while swirling wine around in jewel-encrusted goblets or having their fingers washed by pre-teen boys also wearing dresses, I entertained myself by looking at the assembled Sicilians and hangers on. It took a while for the priest to complete all that introductory stuff with the waving about of black silk cloths and raising up of silver and gold plate with more bling than you could find even in the front row of mourners. Then we participated in the prayers and sat as bidden to listen to the priest eulogize the only Mafia don I had ever known.

I figured Big Rosie's given name would be something like Frank, or Carmine, or maybe Vito. Even Vincent. I never expected Alphonse. Alphonse Eugene Melanzane, to be precise.

I never expected that the priest would refer to him as a good family man (maybe the priest was into double entendre) and a beacon of light for the whole community. OK, that I could believe. I saw pictures of his house at Christmas once. Remember the great New York City blackout in 1965? Not the one in 1977 that struck only New York City. The earlier one, on Nov. 9, 1965, that took out most of six states and lots of eastern Canada for several hours that night. Some say it was UFOs. I suspect it was Big Rosie testing his Christmas lights.

At sometime in the recent past, my wife had shown me the video of what Big Rosie created, every year, for Christmas. He put a life-size crèche in the front garden, and above it, attached to the top of a black-painted light pole, but very skinny, was an angel. Not just any angel, a Renaissance angel, all long golden hair, flowing crimson robes and ermine cuffs. I suspected the fur was real.

The entire roof of the house was covered in lights. Conveniently, the Italian flag is pretty good colors for Christmas lights—red, white and green. So that's what color the lights were, just like on the flag. Green on the left, white in the middle, red on the right.

Every window was outlined in lights; guess what colors? In one, there was a lighted portrait of Frank Sinatra, full flesh tones. I think it was a prime example of neon art. You don't think there is such a thing? There is. There is even a museum of neon art. It used to be in Vegas, of course. But it has now moved upscale, to Glendale, CA.

You can even take a neon cruise sponsored by the museum, beginning in Chinatown. It's a bus tour. At night. No neons in the ocean....You can't make this stuff up, as I've noted before.

Neon Sinatra's face glowed when the outdoor speaker system was broadcasting Sinatra's version of "Silent Night." The faces in the other windows went dark. When Doris Day sang "Que

Sera, Sera," her face became illuminated, and the others went dark. When Dean Martin sang "When the Moon Hits Your Eye Like a Big Pizza Pie" (also known as "That's Amore"—love—but I like the longer title better), his face glowed, alone. However, all the faces were illuminated when Andrea Bocelli or Luciano Pavarotti sang "Ave Maria." Big Rosie apparently liked to give the singers equal attention, so he had a little control system that would change the face that was glowing to match the song being played.

All that neon and warbling Christmas cheer wasn't too bad, I imagine, even if you were a close neighbour—and all the neighbors were close in Carroll Gardens, like in an English village. The houses were terraced. But when "Mambo Italiano" came on, watch out! It was by Rosemary Clooney (Irish, go figure), and when it did, all the faces were illuminated, plus there was a little mechanical tableau on the other side of the front walkway that had a bunch of mannequins dressed up like Italian peasants grabbing arms and flinging each other about. It was, of course, spotlighted. On the video, Big Rosie was standing next to the tableau, beaming, with a red rose in his lapel that flashed a red beam in tune to the "Hey" part of the song and then quivered the rest of the time. All this led me to believe that, in Big Rosie's book, Rosemary Clooney was at least as important as Boceli and Pavarotti. Very magnanimous and multi-cultural of him, I thought. Or maybe he just thought Rosemary Clooney was cute. She was, back in the *White Christmas* film days. By 1997, the last time I laid eyes on her, she had gained a girth similar to Big Rosie's, and carried just about as much bling around with her, at least on the telly programme I saw when she appeared in an electric-blue sequined potato sack…and even then, the rolls of flab were evident. To give her credit, though, she told a story on herself. Her doctor, she said, had questioned her about her increase in girth. "Rosemary," he said, "What have you been doing?" I don't know what she actually replied, because I offered my own response, "I've been eating," and my wife punched me, so then I had to scream Ouch!

The priest's eulogy was just about as oversized as Rosemary Clooney in her later years, and Big Rosie's Christmas Extravaganza every year. He referred to Big Rosie's generosity to his community, to the helping hand he had given the church itself. Big Rosie had paid for the construction of the basement refurbishment, and he had supervised the pouring of the cement for the basement extension himself.

Big Rosie always sponsored a local baseball team for young people, the priest noted. I noted that it was good advertising to have Melanzane Cement Overcoats on the backs of the jerseys. (It didn't really say that. It said Melanzane Construction, Inc.) But Big Rosie didn't have to spring for the end-of-season party for all the players and their families. Nor did he have to contribute so heavily to the Injured Jockeys Fund for riders hurt not only at the New York race tracks, but no matter where they were hurt, how, or why.

Finally, Big Rosie was an exemplary churchgoer. He had been an usher, always ready to help newcomers, old people, anyone. He had never missed a service on a Sunday unless he was out of town, and he was often in the pews on weekday mornings, as well, his rolled up newspaper by his side, waiting for one or another of his friends to join him. Afterwards, he never stopped to chat, as he did on Sundays; it was important to Big Rosie to get his day off to a holy start, and put the wheels in motion to deliver more loads of cement to the gentrification projects going on next door in the Red Hook neighbourhood. Finally, after years of being a horrific ghetto where no self-respecting Italian-American would deign to tread, it was on its way up…with Melanzane Construction pouring foundations for dozens of working-class homes, complete with basements and some with views of the Gowanus Canal. Big Rosie Melanzane's next move, he had told the priest not a month before his death, would be to clean up the Gowanus Canal. He had been working on an exclusive agreement with the city in which he would do ALL the work of cleanup and relining the canal with fresh cement.

I tried not to make those choking noises everyone knows signals disbelief…but still, what better way to ensure that no prosecutor ever find out whose bones might be lying silent and not very deep in the extended rain puddle known as the Gowanus Canal.

Yes, indeed, Big Rosie Melanzane's death was a huge loss to the Italian-American community, and to everyone who crossed its path. At the time, I had no idea how big a loss it was going to be to me.

Actually, I had all I could do to keep from howling with laughter during that long, sad eulogy. Maybe I would have if my wife hadn't grabbed my hand and sunk her blood-red salon-lengthened nails into my flesh. I wanted to scream, or laugh, or both, and my eyes were watering.

On the way out, Double R said he didn't know I cared so much about his father. I guess he had only noticed me when I was in a weepy mood, not when my memories of Big Rosie vis a vis "pillar of the community" made me smirk, smile, and, briefly, even grin.

"I know he wasn't always nice to you," Double R said. "I saw how he warmed up to you after that guy Myron told the donkey story, though. But I didn't think it was enough to make you cry.

I'm touched, really touched," Double R said, patting me on the back and jerking his head in the direction of my handle on Big Rosie's double-wide final slumber chamber. In Sicilian, a head jerk in a particular direction constitutes an invitation. Who needs words?

I grabbed the handle, looked straight ahead, and walked Big Rosie out of his final visit to the church where he doubtless confessed every Saturday to the violations of the Ten Commandments of the week before. I figured commandments five and seven had been his special preserve. That would be the ones about killing and stealing. Of course, I didn't actually KNOW he did either of those things. So by thinking those thoughts in church, was I violating number eight? Was I, in fact, bearing false witness against my neighbour? Nah. You have to speak to bear false witness. You have to speak to lie. In most cases, you have to speak to get someone to whack someone else. Hey...maybe that was why the head jerk had become the communication of choice among the wise guys; if they didn't say a word, they couldn't get nailed for anything.

You also may wonder why I knew the commandments by heart. I mean, who does? Only kids going to Sunday School, I would have thought. But, you might recall, I taught at the College of Unformed Minds and Holy Orders to Do Good (no, not its name either), so I had them memorized. It was sort of subliminal there; they were posted in their entirety at the end of each hallway. It forced me to walk along the hallways like a nerd, head down looking at my shoes, but I caught a glimpse enough times that they sank in. I never liked that one about adultery. Why should some old guy in the desert with a stone tablet have given a bulrush what modern Europeans, Brits and Yanks did for fun?

I thought it was too bad the RCs didn't go in for the Seven Deadly Sins anymore, as I understood they had for a few of the medieval centuries. The church was harder on people who indulged in those, apparently, than on those who violated the Decalogue. (Latin for list of ten...you keep forgetting I am, really, a professor and as pedantic as you like.)

I can't really think of any of the Seven Deadly Sins I wouldn't have pegged Big Rosie for. Wrath? Oh, yeah. I had seen him in a meltdown once...I think it was when someone said something rude about Rosalie, but the expression of the wrath was so intense, it sticks in my mind more than whatever caused it. Big Rosie had hands like malformed pincers of a very large lobster. He reached out, picked up the guy by his shoulders, and drove at least four finger of each hand into the guy's collarbone. I had never seen anyone go grey so fast, but that guy did, and literally slumped to the floor as Big Rosie straightened his shoulders, shook out his arms, pulled on each fat, pink finger as if to stretch it back to shape for the next time, and quietly—very, very quietly—turned around and left the room.

Greed. Yes. Sloth. Well. Hmm... Big Rosie was a pretty well-groomed guy, and to get where he was in the Organization, he had to take care of business. So maybe he gets a pass on sloth.

Pride. Goes without saying. Lust. I never saw it expressed, but I can't imagine an Italian guy, with all those gorgeous young Italian ladies around, not having a twinge now and then. Even America's former President Jimmy Carter admitted to having lust in his heart. Where the hell else would it be?

Envy. If he envied anyone, I would think it was Capone, or maybe one of the lesser Mafia lights. John Gotti maybe. No, it had to be Gambino.

By now, you're wondering how I got to be so familiar with New York City crime families, right? Well, I wasn't always the poster boy for nerdiness. When I was younger, I had friends in low places, one of which was the famous New York newspaper, *Newsday*. One of the writers there had gone to school in England, and we kept in touch. When he grew up and got married and had a child, he was still assigned to his first beat, organized crime, because he was good at it. He was so nerdy looking (birds of a feather, and all that, regarding our friendship), that the crime bosses spilled their guts to him as they would never have done to someone who looked slick. So he wrote a lot about the Gambino family, particularly Thomas Gambino. Gambino had just gotten out of prison, again, when my friend's first kid was born. "Hey, I wanna be da godfatha," Gambino told him. "OK?" My friend said OK. What else could he say? But as I understand it, Gambino didn't actually show up at the christening. Still, my friend has always thought that if his daughter got in big trouble, he had a friend who could give the chump some big trouble right back.

The final deadly sin was gluttony, and chances are, it killed Big Rosie. He was, after all, stuck under the steering wheel of that car. And I'd rather think that, and have Double R think that, than consider the possibility that my unseemly questioning by the constabulary regarding that horrific find in the L car had anything to do with it. I was keeping my fingers crossed. Double R wasn't stupid, but he had only been the new boss-designate of the Melanzanes for a few days and would become the boss of bosses—capo di tutti capi—until or unless the death of Big Rosie caused a sort of Italian faction fight for supremacy, so he might still have had a smudge of the milk of human kindness on him. Heck, Big Rosie was actually kind to me that once. Before he died. Oh, god. I had to stop thinking that way and "carry" the coffin. Which I did.

Then we put it down on the coffin gurney for its final few feet into the waiting, flower-bedecked Cadillac hearse. We turned as if to leave and go to the cars and limos, until we heard the crunch of metal and, as one, turned around. The front wheels of the gurney had buckled, and the coffin, in all its mahogany glory, had slipped its blanket of red roses and was headed south toward the street.

Did you ever see five Mafia guys and a scozza—a jerk—watch a huge mahogany coffin slide down church steps barely missing a couple kids playing cards for money on the kerb? It slipped across the pavement and came to rest with the head of the coffin jammed into the slime moving down the gutter in the rain, the foot pointing toward the sky like the bow of a sinking ship listing to its final resting place on the ocean floor. It was the Titanic, all over again—in all mahogany except or the gold fittings—sinking into dark, viscous ooze that was a Brooklyn street on a hot day. The rose blanket had come apart, and roses were bobbing on the dark ground like so many shipwreck survivors waiting to be plucked from the jaws of death.

All of a sudden, six pallbearers and a half dozen funeral directors were rushing toward the coffin. When it finally stopped in the middle of the road, not 10 feet from a city bus pulling out and a taxi halted to pick up a female passenger who was blanching and emitting high-pitched screams, we got our shoulders under the top end. It was a wonder that, with Big Rosie resident inside, it hadn't splintered into a million pieces, but perhaps the lead liner did some good. Whether or not it would keep him for eternity, it certainly kept him from the ignominy of rolling out on Court Street, Brooklyn, before an astonished—and for once pin-drop silent—crowd of Italian relations, friends and hangers on.

Once we had Big Rosie's coffin stabilised, the priest got a flat-bed yard cart from the shed at the back of the car park. "We use it for rock salt in the winter," he explained. "Those bags are heavy." Then he and a couple of other bystanders wrangled it under the middle of Big Rosie's coffin and we six pallbearers let Big Rosie down onto it. There was no help for it. We could push him close to the hearse on the makeshift gurney, but the six of us were going to have to lift Big Rosie in for his final ride, while a funeral director went to the funeral home for a spare gurney with which to decant him at the other end.

SEVENTEEN

Bad Moon Rising

During the entire sideshow, the congregation was still as statues, standing on the steps watching. You know how people say their mouth dropped open? Well, their mouths really did drop open. You never saw anything like it. It was like a flock of birds, big-eyed and wide-mouthed waiting for a tasty worm to fall in. Not all, though. Some had their mouths covered with their hands. They looked like a platoon of Speak No Evil monkeys on steroids with their wide eyes staring at us.

The funeral directors were good, though. They shepherded those going to the cemetery into the limos, had the drivers turn on the AC and some soothing music, and they began stacking the flowers—an entire Dutch cantonment of flowers—into the hearse.

Most of the flowers were red. As we followed behind, even though we were several cars behind, I caught a glimpse of the hearse at the corners. It looked like a fire was raging in there.

On top, it looked like a rolling garden of garish blooms. I had never seen anything like it. No one from England would ever have seen anything like it. In England, there will be a hearse, maybe a limo for the immediate family, but everyone else drives their own cars to the cemetery. I thought it was the same, or at least similar, in America. But I was wrong, at least for dead Mafia dons.

There was a lead limo in which the funeral directors sat. It was topped by a huge display of flowers, like half a wreath with spiky things coming out of it reaching for the sky. Then there was the hearse, filled inside with Big Rosie's final red roses, and an even bigger spray of roses sitting on top. There must have been a thousand roses in that hearse crown, maybe more.

The next car was one holding all the flowers that wouldn't go in the hearse. On top of that, another spray, only this one was multicoloured like the first, with arms of flowers draped off each side and almost hitting the ground. No wonder the pace was set at ten miles per hour.

Still, the ride to the cemetery was relatively uneventful. Because we were in the last "family" car, and only Chloe and an old deaf guy were riding with us, my wife got to tell me a lot about the scenery. Take the Gowanus Canal, for example, that we had to cross to get to St. John's Cemetery in Queens, the county next to Brooklyn, except the cemetery is run by the Roman Catholic Diocese of Brooklyn. Hey…this is New Yawk!

The Carroll Gardens neighbourhood was right next to the Gowanus neighbourhood. And both were early and heavily Italian, and both had organized crime early on.

"There are a lot of stories about people who got whacked and dumped into the Gowanus Canal," my wife said. "Early in the 20th century, there was a street brawl that got started when two rival undertakers fought over who got to bury the body of a kid who fell in and drowned."

"He drowned?" I asked. "The thing looks solid to me."

"It almost is. The only body of water in New York that will burn," she said. "All the maritime fuel in it. And stiffs."

Then she clammed up. The old deaf guy spoke. I guess he wasn't that deaf. "Including her father," he said, pointing a bony claw in my wife's direction.

I looked at her. She had told me her father and mother had both died when she was a teenager, just before she want off to college, and she had been given a home to come back to by Big Rosie and Rosalie from that point on. I never asked how her parents had died; she always clammed up when the subject arose and I didn't like to pry.

But now she was crying. That's all right. It was a funeral. But Chloe had her arm around my wife, and was searching in her purse with the other hand for a tissue. I handed my wife my clean white handkerchief, the one she had provided for me every single day of our marriage, and which I almost never used. I have good mucus membranes; no need. I didn't wear a silk suit, so there was no need for a pocket square. I guess it was just her thing.

My wife blew her nose. I looked a question at her.

"I guess I should tell you. My father's body was found floating in the Gowanus Canal. My mother never got over it; she died of a broken heart a month later. A month after that, after Big Rosie and Rosalie had given me a home—when I turned 18—I decided to apply for British citizenship because my mother was British. It had nothing to do with my ex-husband," she said. "I lied," she added, in a wee, small voice. My heart melted.

"I don't know why his body was floating," she added. "He was just an accountant for a construction company out on Long Island. Sure, he was Big Rosie's cousin. Not his brother; we just called Big Rosie my uncle because he was always around when I was little, and he paid for my father's university classes so he could become an accountant. That's how he left me so much money. It wasn't really my ex-husband. He was a bum. It was my father. He made good investments."

Chloe wasn't speaking, and her face was a blank. Almost a blank. There was something she didn't quite believe, but wasn't ready to talk about. I knew that look. I had known if for a long time, a miniscule tightening of her upper lip, an infinitesimal squinting of her eyes, and a hint of a leftward head tilt.

"On the ponies," the deaf old guy said.

"What?" Chloe asked.

"You know, he had a gambling jones," the deaf old guy said. "He was always at the track. He was hardly ever at the construction company. He made all his money at the track. That's what pissed off Big Rosie."

Blank stares from me and my wife. Chloe took out her handkerchief, covered her nose with it, blew a ladylike blast, and turned her head toward the window. She turned it way left, and I was fairly certain the lips were tightening and eyes narrowing and she didn't want me to see. I just didn't know why.

"He died from it," the old deaf guy said. "The track. Sure. Ask Big Rosie. He'll tell you."

"But Big Rosie…." I began, before Chloe nudged me in the shins hard with her pointy-toed patent leather court shoes.

"Good idea," Chloe said. "But what should we ask him in particular?" Chloe was not about to tell him, as I had been, that it was Big Rosie's funeral we were attending. Figures. It was her business to let people talk until they spilled what she wanted to hear. But I wondered, did the guy have Alzheimer's? Could we believe anything he said?

My wife was shivering. I reached across and stroked her knee; we were sitting across from each other, with Chloe across from the old deaf guy. I had never seen my wife shiver before, at least not from anything except the rising damp in England. She was so steadfast most of the time, all of the time. Until now. Maybe it was all part of the thaw I had seen when Miracle showed up.

Miracle! Holy cow, I hadn't even thought of the poor girl for days and days. I wondered if she was out of the coma yet. And what about the Jadrool twins? And Bulpitt.

Here I was, having the time of my life at a rip-roaring Mafia funeral, and Miracle might be in need of a friendly face. Bulpitt might be in need of my fist in his face. And the Jadrool family...well, who the heck cared about the Jadrool family. I let those thoughts rumble for a minute or two, as the old deaf guy finished his deep-lung hacking so he could go on with whatever he was going to tell us.

"Ask Big Rosie about that horse that broke its leg."

"Which one?"

"Not the one in the Triple Crown. A year later."

"Oh, that one."

"Yup," the old geezer said. "That one. Knobbled. Big Rosie got by with it that time."

"And?"

"And I'm done talking. Just ask Big Rosie. He'll tell you. Frankly, it's a miracle he lived this long. And that other guy...his nephew? He took the hit on that one, I guess."

And then the old guy with senile dementia and no idea whose funeral he was attending—maybe funerals were his hobby for all we knew—clammed up. My wife just sat gazing out the window as if she wanted to fly out of the car, run off into the stream of headlights coming toward us in the rain that had kicked up on our way down the parkway, and disappear. I couldn't blame her. She had told me...well, not told exactly, but indicated...that while some of her family sort of seemed to be Mafia, her own family was just another ordinary Italian-American family from Brooklyn, NY. And I believed it. Gullible.

Still, I wasn't at all annoyed by all of this, oddly enough. I mean, my wife was my wife. The woman who very occasionally cooked me a meal, who provided riches beyond my wildest imaginings….What, I wondered, would happen to those riches now? Apparently, my wife's supposed alimony was really guilt payments from Uncle Big Rosie. At least, that's what I got out of the disjointed tale the old guy told. There was no rich ex-husband.

Well, there was an ex-husband, but probably not rich. Good thing I had a job, I thought. Money might be a little tight without Big Rosie to send care packages full of American greenbacks. I wondered how we were going to pay for all that ice they had bought for the funeral. It wasn't like we had a big honking chunk of it like the one pinned to Rosalie's dress to sell if the need arose. Quite a stone, that was. Big Rosie must have left her a pile.

My wife continued staring into the rain and shivering. Chloe looked thoughtful. The old deaf guy went to sleep, but I had plenty of time to think as we were all mired in the urban crawl in the rain to the cemetery in far-off Queens.

EIGHTEEN

Not Fade Away

I must say, the incident at the church sort of calmed the family down a bit, or shocked them. Or maybe it was the sudden rainstorm, complete with thunder and bolts of lonely lightning looking for electrical wires to thrill. Either way, it meant there was less wailing than I expected at the gravesite, so I got a good look around as we stood in the cemetery getting drenched, although shielded a bit by the big green awnings the funeral directors had hurriedly erected over the chairs where the family were seated. There were a couple of New York's finest staked out, watching the crowd, I swear. I'd have been surprised if there weren't. It was, after all, a mob funeral, even if a minor branch of whatever family tree the Melanzanes had climbed down out of. It paid to know the enemy, I guess.

For all the NYPD knew, the late Alphonse Eugene Melanzane might be the successor to the guy he was going to do his Dirt Nap next to, Carmine "The Doctor" Lombardozzi. The late Mr. Lombardozzi had been dozing for a while, since Sept. 5, 1992, in fact. (I looked all this up online later.) He was a big cheese in the Gambino family, a capo (captain) who ran the loan sharking rackets. There's a lot of money in money. Remember Rocky Balboa, the Philly boxing bum who made it big? He was an enforcer for loan sharking, breaking people's legs and things of that nature. Mr. Lombardozzi didn't do the actual leg-breaking; he employed a Rocky or two. But when he was young, breaking legs would have been the least of his anger-management issues.

He was discharged from the US Army during WWII because of his psychopathic behaviour. Zowie! He ended up dying of a heart attack at age 79, about a dozen year after the Feds indicted him for tax problems, specifically, failing to declare the income from his loan sharking business.

I thought Inland Revenue was dumb. But imagine any nation thinking its criminals would report their income from their illegal businesses. It boggled my mind. Apparently, the United States uses its revenue collection arm, the Internal Revenue Service, a lot like the Mafia uses its Rocky Balboa's, as enforcers. There is a difference, of course, and I shall find it, I'm sure, if I am ever dumb enough to take up residence Stateside. My wife has had to pay income taxes there forever; the U.S. doesn't let anyone out from under just because they live, work and earn in a different country. Two nations on earth try to extract coinage from those who once lived there—in the case of the US, even foreigners who once worked in the US before returning home, I kid you not. Those two nations are the US, and Liberia. Figures. Liberia was founded by former US slaves in about 1820. Its government is modelled on that of the US. Ergo….

But I digress again. Still, the foibles of the colonists never cease to amuse me. I researched Lobardozzi after we got home, and nowhere could I find out if Lombardozzi was tried and convicted, or tried and acquitted. Nothing. Maybe he bought the justice system. On that thought, I had begun to shiver as badly as my wife had at the funeral. Was I at large in a brave new world of some sort? A parallel universe? Or had the old Wild West been recreated and updated with cars instead of horses and big, fat, cigar-chomping Italian guys instead of lean, mean, cigarillo-smoking gunslingers?

Yes, my imagination was getting away from me. But what do you expect when my brain was busy at every spare moment matching up the notes and money we had found in Big Rosie's coat, with what Rosie did for a living, with all that money my wife kept getting in wire transfers that were NOT from her ex-husband, but from her late uncle. Indeed, all this occupied my mind from right after the funeral, when I had a brief online session in the hotel room—just me and Google and Wikipedia.

All too soon, it seemed, the interment was over, and we had picked our way back to the cars, dodging each other's umbrellas. Rosalie and her son and daughter-in-law left first, Rosalie still crying and leaving a trail of tissues behind her like Hansel and Gretel and the bread crumbs...although the tissues would last longer than crumbs, if not longer than stones.

Speaking of which, I wondered what Big Rosie's headstone would be like. The Mafia ones tended to be ornate, like a capodimonte fruit bowl gone mad and turned to marble. Indeed, they were almost never a plain grey slab incised with names and dates and maybe a "beloved husband of...". They often had shades of grey, even pink. Lots of interesting little angels. Maybe the angels were a sort of subliminal message to God: See these? That's where we want this guy's soul to go? Kapisch? We already told the priest, and he's gonna tell you too. OK? OK.

It could be worse, though. The Russian mob erects laser-etched, full-height black marble tombstones with a portrait of the stiff as he was in life, drinking, carousing or whatever.

But the sentiments were the same as any family man's: Beloved husband and father, and then the dates. That's what Big Rosie's said; nowhere did it say he was a "made man."

I didn't know if Big Rosie was a made man, but he must have been to have a funeral of such magnitude.

I hoped Big Rosie wasn't turning in his grave. So far, no one had suggested that it was in running after me that Big Rosie suffered his heart attack and died. I thought that might be the case, but I certainly wasn't going to mention it. Things had been going so well.

The family hadn't actually accepted Chloe, but they hadn't rejected her either. Double R was being fairly friendly to me. Cousin Tommy and spouse simply ignored me. My wife was beginning to reveal the truth underlying her uncompromising insistence on always looking good, and factors beyond her control were beginning to reveal what sort of hornet's nest I had got myself into when I married a person I had thought was a rich American divorcee. Even visually, I had slipped through a portal someplace to another world.

The stoic men attending the funeral all wore black suits and dark ties. Some older men wore off-white cashmere topcoats with fur collars. The younger men eschewed the topcoats, but they had left no stone unturned in adding heavy gold rings to their ensemble, as well as gold and diamond cuff links and a few sported gold tie clasps as well. Among the women, black was the colour of choice, and diamonds the jewellery of choice. Most wore hats like one sees at an English wedding—all wide-brimmed and decked out with flowers and feathers sprouting at odd angles—but in black, just black. No colours at all. Indeed, if not for the varied hair colours under the hats and the flowers on the funeral cars, you would have thought you were in a 1940s gangster film.

Welcome to my world.

NINETEEN

Up, Up and Away

All too soon, the fun family festivities were at an end. Unlike the Irish in New York, the Italians do not have a roisterous lunch or dinner after the interment. The widowed spouse goes home, accompanied by his or her children and their families, and everyone else goes where everyone else goes.

We went to Lucali. We barely got our slice, the line to get in was so long. But it was worth it. It's supposed to be the best pizza in Brooklyn, and I thought it was. We all did. But what did I know? The only one of us who could even eat pizza properly was my wife, since she grew up in Carroll Gardens. What, you might ask, is the proper way to eat pizza? Isn't it OK as long as you get the delightful mess of bread, olive oil, cheese and tomato sauce into your gob? No. To qualify as a world-class pizza eater, that is, a Brooklyn, NY pizza eater, you have to take the wedge, pick it up in your right hand, fold it in half using only your thumb and forefinger, and shove the point into your face. If olive oil drips down your chin, that's OK. But never—NEVER—eat pizza in Brooklyn with a knife and fork. You'll be laughed at. I know this for a fact. Chloe did not get laughed at; she followed my wife's lead.

You don't believe me? Here are two real, live comments on the internet on Serious Eats in answer to the question of whether to eat pizza with a knife and fork or not. Here they are:

- FOLD IT or else. that's like eating a hamburger with a fork and knife.... it's just not done!

- The only way to eat pizza is to fold it up and go
  nuts. I have an ex-bf who used to eat his pizza with
  a knife and fork (also cut up all his pasta into tiny
  pieces) and I'm pretty sure it was in the top ten
  reasons of why we broke up.

You're never too old to learn something. At Lucali, I learned
what ~~good~~ great pizza really is, and got the last word on how to
eat it.

The letdown of leaving world-class pizza behind combined
with excitement at going home—tempered by a bit of
understandable angst on my part—kicked in when we left Lucali.
We were all getting on a plane that evening to go back home,
where we would find out how Miracle was, whether the cops had
identified the second body, what Bulpitt was up to, and if we
were in line for attendance at another funeral, Mrs. Bulpitt's.
Two weeks is about right in the UK between death and a funeral,
and often there is a relatively quiet luncheon afterward.

But first, we had to deal with Homeland Security and the
TSA. No, it doesn't stand for Trashy Stupid Assholes, although it
might as well. In fact, they make rent-a-cops—even Myron
Lillicrap—look like paragons of virtue and tact, and pinnacles of
intellectual achievement. Not one of us wanted to subject our
bodies to the full-body scan machine, which meant we were
pulled aside and told to wait for the groping to commence. That's
not exactly how they said it, but we had all read news reports.

"Do you think it will tickle?" my wife asked.

"No, I think you'll be too pissed off to be tickled."

"Will it be embarrassing?"

"Of course. That's their intention, I think. And it proves how
stupid they are. A real terrorist wouldn't be embarrassed; if
you've already decided to blow up 400 people, there isn't a

whole lot that would embarrass you. So, as I said, it's an exercise in embarrassment for all us regular folks with nothing to hide."

Chloe laughed.

It was true, though. I had nothing to hide. My wife had nothing to hide, at least nothing that I knew about then.

So we went through the motions of being patted down. Some guy ahead of me was screaming about touching his junk. I wouldn't call mine junk. I know four women, at least, who wouldn't call mine junk. Maybe the passengers were as stupid as the grope squad.

When it came my turn, I naturally decided to entertain the sour-looking gentleman assigned to assess the tenor of my tendons, the mass of my musculature, the bulkiness of my bones, the fullness of my fat. I said, "Repeat after me," and cleared my throat. I cleared it loudly several times. I then described a circle in the air with my right hand, using two fingers to poke the eyes, one finger to describe the length of nose, and one finger again to make a smiley mouth in the air.

The TSA goon didn't know what to do. Soon, I realized the other goons had ceased their work, hands poised in mid-air—not unlike my own—over some grannie's Depends area, checking for wetness, a smuggled bottle of grain alcohol, or maybe plastique, three things most old ladies will try to conceal by wearing Depends and looking like they have a load in their polyester pants.

Apparently, my personal frisker wasn't feeling frisky at all. He bellowed, "Supervisor" until a hulking human with an Aztec face and ballerina hands came running. She just looked at me.

"What?"

She continued to stare, and I got the feeling she was calling up some Aztec demon named something like Peplepotacatl

Xlabacatl. "If you wouldn't mind stepping over to the side," she said, in a tone that meant do it or else. So I did. I don't know what got into me. Maybe it was Peplepotacatl Xlabacatl. She asked me if I had had too much to drink. No. Taken any drugs? No. Smoked any dope? No. Looking for a way to be detained in the US for a while? Lord No. No. A thousand times no. Look, I had a really great time at the funeral, but the place had been trashed by its bankers and its former head of state even more than the UK had. "No, ma'am," I said, suddenly sober in every way. "I was just trying to lighten up the process a bit."

"So you're a comedian?"

"No, a driving instructor."

"Same difference," she said in what I had learned was a common Brooklyn oxymoronic response. She motioned Frisker Man to finish the pat-down ASAP and get me out of there. Fine with me. I was hardly fifty feet behind my wife and Chloe when I got through. Both of them rolled their eyes at me.

"What?" I shrugged at them. I was learning really fast how to be a New Yorker. Maybe I should have taken the nice lady up on her offer to stay.

Once I was through the barrier, I waited until my frisker turned in my direction. I smiled and described the "happy face" in the air again. Then I cleared my throat, loudly, several times and made the happy face again. I smiled.

He smiled back. He laughed. He finally got it. Ah. Good deed for the year out of the way. I had made a total stranger laugh. Things could be worse.

And they were. Six hours' worth of worse over the Atlantic, wedged into a metal tube, almost pinioned to tiny perches that scarcely let one's butt cheeks expand to accommodate a fart. Just as well; air filtration in airplanes isn't as good as they'd like you to think it is. Not that I'm squeamish. Did you know that James Joyce was apparently addicted to his wife's farts? The infamous Nora Barnacle of Galway must have smelled better than the fish-based Irish diet would lead one to believe. Joyce immortalized those farts in a letter, thus:

I think I would know Nora's fart anywhere. I think I could pick hers out in a roomful of farting women. It is a rather girlish noise not like the wet windy fart which I imagine fat wives have. It is sudden and dry and dirty like what a bold girl would let off in fun in a school dormitory at night. I hope Nora will let off no end of her farts in my face so that I may know their smell also.

I'm not going to cite that. Just google it; you can find it in dozens of places on the internet, which just goes to show, people like to pretend they don't enjoy scatology, but they're lying.

Anyway, we got ourselves settled in the tiny perches crammed into the metal tube. We didn't talk much. What was there to say? We all knew that the funeral had been an entertaining interlude in what was doubtless going to be a taxing time after we got home.

Still, it would be good to be home, I thought.

But I was wrong. It wasn't that all hell had broken loose in our absence, just most of hell.

We found out about the hell because I no sooner stepped off the plane than my mobile began to vibrate like a pole dancer with jock itch; there were messages from Miracle. Lots of them. So at least we knew she was all right. I looked at the messages as we waited in the baggage hall. That's how I found out that:

First, the police knew who the second body was.

Second, Bulpitt was missing and presumed dead. Nah, not the last part. That was just my wishful thinking. But he had gone missing.

Third, Miracle had indeed been poisoned by belladonna. And they had found some in my house.

Could it get any worse? I mean, how did they get into my house? How did they serve a warrant and enter when I was gone? I asked Chloe.

"Simple. They weren't able to communicate with you, and they had reason to believe that there would be evidence in your house connected with grievous bodily harm to Miracle. And possibly they connected the letter addressed to you that was found in the L car with one or more of the cases. Frankly, Shelf, you're in so deep, it almost doesn't matter what the police seek a warrant for, you'll provide it."

"What cases? I'm not involved in cases."

"Shelf, you are involved in the drippers case. You may be involved in something Big Rosie was doing in England without knowing it; have you forgotten the stuff we found in his overcoat? HIDDEN in his overcoat? And what about your criminal student from Africa?"

"Who said he was a criminal?"

Chloe rolled her eyes, murmured uh-huh, one born every minute, stuff like that.

"In any case, the police can legally break and enter, as they obviously did," she said.

I wondered if they then had to find a way to lock it up again, or if all our household goods had been liberated by roving gangs of toughs. Not that there were many in the neighbourhood where we lived, but one never knows.

Although we did know for sure fairly soon. There was nothing missing. At least not as far as our bleary eyes could tell after the Red-Eye from NYC. We got in at 8 a.m. after a night attempting Hindu ascetic self-denial positions in the re-engineered baby chairs that passed for adult seating even on transatlantic flights these days. Maybe they're a good thing. The risk of deep-vein thrombosis probably keeps annoying old farts from flying and disturbing the rest of us with their snoring and loud farts. (No James Joyce, I.) Which leaves only the unsupervised children behind you kicking the back of your seat for six hours while their parents unaccountably remain fast asleep, or are darn good actors. Maybe the kid-kick vibration helps allay deep-vein thrombosis, though. As for the food, I will quote from a letter sent to the (be)knighted owner of one of the UK's great people-moving-flying-metal-tube companies, just the section referring to a packaged sweet of some sort:

> It appears to be in an evidence bag from the scene of a crime. A CRIME AGAINST BLOODY COOKING. Either that or some sort of back-street underground cookie, purchased off a gun-toting maniac high on his own supply of yeast. You certainly wouldn't want to be caught carrying one of these through customs.

Google it. It went viral on YouTube, so much so that the author became a food consultant to the airline in question. I think issuing creative complaints these days is the new contest-entry hobby. Remember that? Back in the 80s and 90s, women—mainly, not to be sexist—used to sit around entering the "Win a Trip to Myanmar" contests and claimed to have added greatly to the family coffers, the family lifestyle, and very possibly the profits of pharmaceutical companies giving them all those jabs for travelling healthily in, as they once were known, Third World countries looking to ride advertising coattails into the First World.

We hadn't had a meal. Not since the slice at Lucali. We had tried to fill the voids in our stomachs with bottled water, the only thing that seemed safe to ingest on the plane after a few days in New York where the food is, to put it mildly, lots more interesting than in my little corner of East Anglia, and a universe beyond airplane cuisine, to be oxymoronic about it. NY food is not necessarily better; the standard of cooking in the UK post-Jamie Oliver is quite good. But where else but NYC can you choose between an Argentine restaurant, a Uighur restaurant, and Bukharian kosher all within walking distance? We skipped the Uighur place, even though I don't think it is legal to eat camel in NYC.

Hungry or not, we had some problems to figure out. I was fairly certain that the constabulary would be after me, having tossed my house—and toss it they had. Luckily, our eyes were so bleary we couldn't even think about straightening the place up right then. But no matter. It's likely no one had stolen our shit because they couldn't tell what was what in the mess. We couldn't. I was contemplating calling ReFurnish to just come get it all, or hiring a cleaning service, or sleeping for about a week and tackling it myself, when the doorbell rang.

Ah, I realized even through the fog, it was doubtless the timely appearance of Her Majesty's local enforcers. They were garbed somewhat differently from my imaginings of medieval thugs in tunics and funny helmets and smelling like Tavistock's Goosey Fair in the old days, when they actually had some geese. Two of East Anglia's finest, in spiffing uniforms despite the blasting summer heat of at least 18° C., walked up to the door almost as soon as we got our coats off, my wife and I. Chloe had gone on home, after dropping us off; she had driven us all to the airport, a kindness, considering.

There were no handcuffs involved, and the coppers weren't nasty about it, but they did say my wife should expect me to be gone for a while. Why didn't they take my wife along? It was her belladonna. It had to be, because it wasn't mine. And besides, after Miracle's message, I had asked my wife about it. Surprise! She said it was indeed hers; that she got prescriptions for it because of her travel sickness issues. There was so much I hadn't known about her, having been bowled over at the time by her physical attractions, and having relapsed into my old boorish Shelf persona shortly after the wedding. (That was over now. I was in love with my wife, she is a wonderful woman. So there.) But still, I hadn't noticed any such issues on the way to NYC or back. And I hadn't known, obviously, about the belladonna. I was wondering how much more I didn't know about my wife that would throw a spanner into the works sooner or latter. But I kept my yap shut.

"Of course you didn't notice any issues as you call them, you dolt," she said, unkindly I thought after the warming up she had done, and I had done, under the most taxing of circumstances. "I keep a couple of doses in my purse in case I should need them. They are prescription. From a *bona fide* NHS family PHYSICIAN. Okay? And I TOOK SOME a couple of times when I went to POWDER MY NOSE. *OKAY*?" I didn't like the yelling.

And I wondered how often she had thought she was going to find herself on an airplane or a boat, but I didn't ask. I have made it my religion to avoid intimate knowledge of the precautions a woman might make to cope with what my wife—and Chloe for that matter—still condescendingly refer to as the man's world they are forced to live in. They must have other men than me in mind. I have certainly never caused a problem for a woman, at least that she knew about. Nor have I ever forced a woman to do anything. I can't even get a woman to cook me a single slice of black pudding for love nor money; stands to reason there's precious little Shelf Barker could do to force a woman to do anything. Despite the pressures of the moment, I pondered my own inadequacies. But still, the mysteries of my wife's mysteries was getting to me.

As for the cops, how would they know who put the belladonna in Miracle's wine? It could have been anybody. Anybody who was in the house at the time. So again…why didn't they invite my wife in for a chat, too? I wasn't going to suggest it. I admit, before all this began—when I was still, as the femi-nazis say, objectifying her—I might have suggested it. But I had come to know my wife much better over the past week or so, and it turns out she really is the gem I thought she was the first time I saw those luscious lips, perfect figure and lustrous hair. Only now I was beginning to appreciate her for other things than just her raw physical beauty, impressive as it was. She was vulnerable. Most men like that. I guess I do, too. And I would protect her, as well as I was able. But she had brains, sensitivity, and inner strength I had never given her credit for. Not her fault. Not at all. I'm man enough to admit I was a jerk. Sometimes.

Chloe had grown on me, too, over the past week. I would never feel about her as I did about my wife—my current wife, and possibly final one. Chloe was in no way vulnerable. But I had to admit, now, that some of the problems in our marriage were possible partly my fault. Oh, all right. They were probably all my fault. But now we were finding friendship, and not a moment too soon. I had a feeling that we—my wife and I—were going to need Chloe's services pretty soon, even more than I had needed them already.

TWENTY

We Are Family

I never realized how much I missed my job until I had sat for another couple of hours being interviewed by the East Anglia constabulary. It was soothing, actually, dealing with some of those nutjobs masquerading as students. Especially compared to dealing with the anomie-causing scripting of the law enforcement officers.

As I sat again in that cold green airless room, I longed for a couple of good—or bad, as the case may be—driving students. I craved their wackiness, even that which was revealed only in minor ways. There was one student who refused to use directional indicators because he thought he might confuse other drivers if he changed his mind before making a turn. I pointed out to him that his attitude was likely to get him broad sided but he also thought that if another driver was following so closely they would slam into him before realizing what he was doing, it served them right. How do you argue with that sort of mentality? I had tried pointing out that he was likely to suffer more damage from a side impact than the other car, but he was stuck in his belief, which didn't change, not even after he had failed ten or so driving tests. Or maybe more. I knew of ten of his failures because he'd taken the test twice with me and with four other Cars from 'L instructors. I laughed aloud when I thought of that and, figuring the officers doubtless watching me from the other side of the one-way window caught it, I waved and smiled.

Another student thought a dual carriage way was a George carriageway. Before you ask…I have no idea why.

Still another called a normal street a single dual carriageway. I'm quite sure that student must have worked for the government. It is such perfect bureaucratese. Very unlike what was happening in my life at the moment, between my Walter Mitty-like daydreams.

In due course, the good cop and the bad cop returned.

"You had no idea, then, that your wife had a prescription for belladonna?" the bad cop snarled.

"No. I have no idea about a lot the things my wife has, does, is...."

"You live together?" he asked.

"Yes. But until recently, we inhabited different worlds. Hers was sort of global, and mine was sort of....of...."

"Circumscribed?" added the good cop. Well, anyway, the bright cop. I didn't expect a two-quid word out of a lowly copper's mouth. But yes, I told him. It had been circumscribed, mainly by the highways and byways of East Anglia, the inanities and insanities of driving students, and my own unwillingness to engage with the world at large. I figured my years at the University of Celestial Blessedness and Baby Cherubs had burned me out. Or maybe it was the meditation and yoga. It couldn't have been the dogs that made me the way I am. I'd hazard a guess that it was a combination of the excesses of western pseudo-religion and ersatz eastern spirituality that did me in. But you can think what you like, of course.

"So tell me about the funeral in Brooklyn, New York." This from the good cop. The bad cop was sitting against the wall, chair tipped back. I hoped, I must admit, that the rear legs would slip and I'd get a nice slapstick moment out of it to add to my tale, but my luck wasn't that good.

Still, I couldn't help smiling, but I was smiling at another thought entirely, although it might have been a sort of two-layer thought cake. My main thought was of the casket careening down the church steps. I thought about Double R's son keeping his eyes to himself despite temptation that would have to be confessed; that was actually sort of charming. I thought about the great food. The great pizza. The bad cop sat forward and asked me if I thought death was amusing.

I assured him I didn't, but for his own education, he'd need to go to a Mafia funeral somewhere. He would begin to understand how these people could be good family men and good made men all at once. And how their wives and kids loved them. How the community loved them. Hell, even the US Armed Forces loved them, or at least, loved Alphonse Eugene Melanzane enough to send a Naval honour guard. I told them all of it. Well, most of it. I left out the bleeding statue. And how my edge of the casket was somewhat lower, despite my height, than the other five portions hefted by the beefier men. I have my pride.

"Mr. Barker, at the moment, we have two decedents that we know of. One was the wife of your boss; the other is a colleague of yours. They were found in the L car you often use, and letters of yours were found with the bodies," the bad cop said.

"A letter."

"The driving school's receptionist fell into a coma at your house after drinking wine you had poured for her out of a bottle on your table brought by your relatives."

"Not mine; my wife's."

"Yes. And then one of your relatives..."

"My wife's..."

"Died after hearing a story told by one of your former students who is now a security guard in the local hospital despite his vow to you—as you mentioned earlier—to return to Cornwall and go into the catering business."

"Go BACK into the catering business."

"In addition, your boss has disappeared. Belladonna was found in your house while you were at a Mafia funeral in another country."

"All true. So why haven't you arrested me?"

"To tell you the truth," the copper said, "We can't arrest you because we would look too stupid. There is simply too much going on around you for you to be any part of it. In short, you are clueless, and when we arrest clueless people, we rarely have the right party. I'll grant you that arresting you might flush them out…they'd feel safe and get careless. But it isn't worth it. It just isn't. So if you could go some way toward enlightening us as to the various relationships involved here, we would find it very helpful."

That's not exactly what he said, but I'm not a parrot.

So I tried to straighten the cop out. I told him that the late Alphonse Eugene Melanzane was my wife's first cousin once removed. He looked blank. "She called him Uncle, but he wasn't her father's brother; he was her father's cousin."

Double R was my wife's second cousin. I think. Well, he was Big Rosie's son. Cousin Tommy was nothing to my wife, I thought, since he was Double R's cousin on his mother's side. As for the Jadrools, I had no idea.

The constable, however, seemed put out at that.

"How can you have no idea who the Jadrools….excuse me, who the Ferraris are?

Ferrari? All that time at the funeral, on the plane…I had not found out the Jadrools' real name. Ferrari. I wondered how someone built more like a rundown Fiat could have a name like that. Ermenigildo and Proserpina Ferrari. Never heard of them, I assured him.

Miracle, I told him, was no relation, just a colleague and friend. Bulpitt was no relation, just a boss and jackass. Mrs. Bulpitt was NOT my lover. Whether she was Ignatz Ignatowski's lover was open to conjecture. I had neither seen nor heard that evil, so I certainly couldn't speak it. Ignatz? A colleague. A nice guy.

"Chloe?"

"She's my ex-wife."

"But she went to your current wife's funeral with you?" The good cop was genuinely surprised. I think. Or a good actor.

"They're just good friends," I said, crossing my fingers. They were, now, though so I needn't have crossed digits. "You know she's a detective?"

"Private investigator, yes," he said. "Have you hired her for something?"

I told him no, but I had sought her advice about how to deal with all this Mafia upheaval in a mild-mannered driving instructor's life.

"And she told you, what?" bad cop asked.

"To be myself, to tell the truth."

"Yes. And have you?"

"Yes."

"To which?"

I smiled.

"To be honest, I've had a sort of epiphany because of all this." I felt I could use words like that because the good cop had. "I have gained a new appreciation for my wife, and my ex-wife. Well, at least this ex-wife."

The good cop smiled. The bad cop looked like he wanted to play a hard game of health club handball, using my head to smash against the backboard.

"Your ex-wife is actually a pretty good detective, and part of the reason we didn't charge you to begin with. Everything we heard from your boss, the evidence in the car, you taking flight a couple of times...," the good cop said, while the bad cop glowered.

How did they know that?

"Anyway, she has been helping us out with this, too."

She hadn't told me. Figures.

"Your wife has also been helping us. Your current wife." The bad cop got up and walked out of the room.

I wondered if any more of my wives were involved. And maybe my old schoolteacher, and I had a distant cousin someplace. Why didn't they just post my troubles on Facebook?

"So what do you want from me?" I asked.

"We would like you to go back to your students tomorrow, and in particular, we would like you to teach a man from Africa who calls himself Abidemi."

Well, I'll be damned. Captain Africa WAS up to something.

"And then I want you to pull a manoeuvre like you did with that Arab guy. Break his nose if you want...."

How much did they know about me, anyway? OK. They could have gotten this from Chloe; it had happened long enough ago that we were still married to each other.

"And then use your mobile to call us. Use this number."

"Why am I doing this?"

"He was involved in getting semi-blood diamonds into this country, and back out to eastern Europe for cutting and polishing. We aren't certain of the mule he used to bring them back. But we are fairly certain a relative of your wife's was involved, in case you're wondering why we didn't invite her for a chat, too. We don't know if she knew—Chloe thinks not—but why take the chance?"

Why indeed, I thought. Was another of my wife's secrets being a smuggled diamond mule? No. I couldn't believe that. I wouldn't believe that. This was the woman I love. Deeply, although suddenly.

It was a lot to take in, and I knew I'd have to spend an entire evening with my wife without spilling the beans, as well. The detective had told me to keep it to myself; "loose lips sink ships" or something to that effect. What to do?

Brainstorm. Call up Chloe and spend the night at her place.

Brain disaster. And tell my wife what? No, I would have to lie. There was no way I could go home, deal with my wife's anxiety and understandable sadness, and carry out a subterfuge against the second-scariest student I had ever had. The Middle Eastern guy whose nose I had broken got top prize on that score; I was just glad he had disappeared into some South London mosque somewhere...or so I assumed. I was fairly certain no fatwa had been issued against me, though. It wasn't hard to find out where I lived. Heck, if you could understand whatever accent she was using, you could find out anything about any of us by smiling at Miracle and asking her.

Miracle! Of course someone had gotten the keys to the L car from her, or if not from her, by pretending to be an auto mechanic or something and asking her where they were kept.

I punched in my home phone number. "I'm sorry, I'm not going to get home tonight," I told my wife. "They said they have lots of questions for me and are giving me a cot at the police station when they're done."

She asked if they were going to arrest me. "No."

She didn't sound convinced, or at least, I thought that's what the heavy sigh meant.

"Really. They just want to know as much as I know about your family."

Wrong. She went silent, too silent. I heard sniffling.

"It's all right," I said. "None of them is here, so they can't be arrested even if they were responsible for the drippers."

More sniffling. I made the right soothing noises, finally, and suggested she call Chloe for some moral support, Miracle to make sure she was OK as a friendly gesture, ditto Rosalie. Then go pick up Mr. Bumpy from the cattery and Biff from the kennel, get a good night's sleep, get up and go shopping, and I'd take us out for a nice dinner tomorrow night. She made murmurs of assent, I spoke some sweet nothings, and we rang off.

The cops really hadn't made an offer of a cot, although it seemed a decent sort of idea. But I was too stunned to ask. So I spent yet another night in the L car. There was one bright spot; when I drove up to the Cars From 'L building in the morning, Bulpitt's car was nowhere to be seen. Maybe he had disappeared for good.

When I went inside, Miracle was not at her post. Some temp was. She didn't have an accent. In fact, she didn't have a personality. Just a well-filled sweater, but not how you think. She'd give Rosalie a run for her money. But I had to hand it to her; she made damn fine coffee, and I needed that—after a bap from a petrol stop and something brownish in a cup for breakfast. Especially when I looked at the schedule and saw that Abidemi was my first student of the day.

I programmed the cop number into my phone, as "Biff," just in case anyone noticed. The dog had to be good for something besides making the odd Circle of Shame and determining how many nights a week I was allowed to take comfort in my marriage. We shared the bed with him. It was never a bother. But I was thinking that might have to change now that I was in love with my wife.

I went to work.

TWENTY-ONE

You Really Got Me

"And how are you today, Mr. Barker," Captain Africa boomed. "I have missed our driving lessons while I was away."

"I thought you were going to buy a license," I said.

"Oh, no, no, no, no," he laughed. "I just was saying that because...I was embarrassed at my lack of skill. A man of my breeding in my country would be thought weak to fail a driving test, that is all. I was ashamed, and so I tried to make it seem like not such a big deal. No, no, no, no, no, Mr. Barker, I will need to take many lessons—many, many lessons—so that I will never fail a driving test again."

Oh, goody, I thought. And then remembered, with any luck, this would be his last driving lesson, if the cops were right. I hoped it wouldn't be my last as well. But, well....I'll get to that.

Anyway, we set off, Abidemi behind the wheel and me a bit distracted since I needed to find a plausible situation in which to use the dual controls to commandeer the car and crash it into something, all without injuring other road users or pedestrians. Health and safety, health and safety. Sure.

About half an hour into the lesson, I realized I would have to find something soon, because he had already pulled to the side once, exited the car, and spent six or seven minutes in his usual dance of conversation and gesticulation. That was actually quite modest for him, and I was certain the interruptions would begin to come more frequently.

And then, there it was. A huge, nasty tanker, milk I thought, poking into the roadway we were on. If it had been a few feet further into our roadway, Abidemi really would have hit it. Really. As it was, I did what I had to do, as any good soldier in the war against…what?…

anyway, in an attempt to carry out the plan the cops had outlined.

It was not a milk tanker. It was filled with a corrosive liquid. OK, we didn't get blown to Edinburgh on a ball of petrol flames; even I would have recognized a petrol tanker. After all, I spent enough time and money buying it for the L cars. But it took a while to get everything squared away. The cops came but had to call a Hazmat team before they could get either one of us out of the car. I couldn't guarantee Abidemi's injuries were much worse than a sore sternum from the seat belt crushing his huge gold pendant into his chest and a split lip. Mine? I thought perhaps I had broken my ankle, but I wouldn't know for sure until I tried to stand.

But Abidemi's briefcase was cracked open like a hazelnut at Christmas. And all over the back of the car were diamonds. At least I think that's what the hunks were, uncut diamonds. I tried not to look at them so that Abidemi wouldn't think anything of it until the cops actually did get to the car. But I failed.

"Mr. Barker, now you know what my business is," Captain Africa said. "And now I am going to have to kill you. It was such a perfect way to receive calls from my contacts. And you were so kind to provide both the mule to get them to the cutters…."

"Me?" I screeched. "Me?"

How?

"Mr. Ignatowski would never have been known to me if you hadn't cancelled my lesson once and substituted him. When I found he needed money badly for his mother's health, well, that was settled."

I didn't want to know what had happened to Iggy. Really.

"And you also provided for me a conduit into the best market, the United States. Mr. Ferrari was so helpful. It is a shame, really, since he has just had two lovely little boys."

I didn't ask. In fact, I hadn't asked anything about them in Brooklyn, nor had I asked my wife since then. But I had a feeling we wouldn't see Jadrool again soon, if ever.

Finally, the cops got us out. Abidemi was relieved of his valuable burden and led away in handcuffs. I was shunted into an ambulance and taken to the Blimey-Gore Hospital.

"No, say it isn't you," the admissions lady said.

I smiled. Right after that, my wife caught up with me, and then Chloe came walking through the door. And Miracle. And Bulpitt.

Huh?

It turned out that Bulpitt had been kept in seclusion by the cops while the mess was sorted out; it had done his disposition no good. On the other hand, he seemed relieved to know that his wife, cheater that she was, had died quickly with a single bullet from Ferrari's gun. She had been Iggy's lover after all, and got whacked along with Iggy when Captain Africa decided to cut his losses because of Big Rosie's interest in entering the diamond trade. Captain Africa proved he was an amateur by hiring Jadrool—that is, Ferrari—not knowing that using a minor Mafioso on the lam would get a real Mafioso involved, Big Rosie. Chalk one up for experience and credentials, even in the killing field.

The necklace was no mystery at all. It had been used by Iggy to ferry small stones back and forth. There was so much filigree work, no one could tell if the stones had been prised out and replaced or not. Mrs. Bulpitt just happened to be wearing it on another tryst with Iggy when Ferrari whacked them.

"Chloe, did you know all this?" I asked.

"Not all of it. But some. When we were in New York, I poked around to see if Big Rosie had gotten into it. Not that it mattered. He was dead. But I thought maybe Double R was involved. As it turns out, he wasn't. He was just taking over the ponies from Big Rosie when all this began to get out of hand."

"So Big Rosie was into horses? How? Fixing races?"

"You could say that," my wife said.

"Sweetheart...."

"No, it's all right. I always knew that the money was not from good investments. I just didn't want to admit it. My father was one of Big Rosie's capos. He tried to get out. And he got out. Permanently. With Big Rosie's help. I think it was guilt that made Big Rosie take care of me. But now Big Rosie is gone so the guilt is gone...which means the money is gone."

Well. So what? I could work.

But she could spend.

I could work a lot.

I had another question. "Who gave Miracle the belladonna?"

"I took it myself," Miracle said. "I was so afraid Mr. Bulpitt was going to frame you for something. I just didn't want to see it. I thought maybe I'd conk out for a bit. I was so stressed from that morning."

Bulpitt looked sheepish. As well he might.

"But I overdid it. And then I nearly got you and Mrs. Barker in trouble. I feel just awful. But Chloe fixed it up. She figured it out when she used the toilet at your house. I guess I hadn't flushed the foil wrap well enough from the bubble-packed medicine. So she fixed that up with the cops for you."

Nice of her. But what about the Jadrools...that is, the Ferraris. How had they got mixed up with the Melanzanes, I wondered. Chloe had the answer.

"The Jadrools were just small-time hoods from New Jersey who decided to see if they could sell Big Rosie on a part of the diamond double-dealing they were into. He said he wanted no part of it. Actually, he was pretty angry. He was about to retire, shift it all to Double R, and have fun in the sun—literally, at a new house in Florida—with Rosalie. He had no interest in getting into a position after all those years where the cops could finger him for something.

"The Jadrools figured it wouldn't be too healthy to have Big Rosie, or even Double R, as an enemy, so they split and came to England. However, they had already involved Big Rosie's favourite niece...and by extension, her husband...by using his colleague Iggy as a mule, recommended by Abidemi. Big Rosie didn't like that, and came over to drag Jadrool over the coals a while. At best. And ensure that you and your wife," she stared at me pointedly, "wouldn't be hurt by any of this."

"So that's why the Jadrools were here already when Big Rosie and company came over," I figured out.

"Shelf, you amaze me. Your gullibility is astonishing. You think even Big Rosie could commandeer a commercial flight and get the lot of them here about ten hours after your wife had called them?" Chloe asked.

"Well, then...."

"Stupido!"

I gave her a glare.

"Stupido. She called his Skype phone. Big Rosie was already here about the diamond stuff and had his Skype phone with him. He didn't want anyone to know where he was; he wanted to surprise the Jadrool."

Suddenly another bulb went off. "Who is the Jadrool' wife?" I asked.

My wife said Mrs. Ferrari was a distant cousin of some sort whose father had also been in the way of Big Rosie's earlier business enterprises and ended up Gowanus-bound.

The Gowanus Canal had long been a dumping ground for excessed hoods. Just one early example is found in a 1936 *New York Times* article, "Body Is Discovered, Bound and Garroted, in Gowanus Waters." It reads: 'Bound and garroted, the body of a man identified early this morning as Tony Gubitosi, 21-year-old petty racketeer of 290 Third Avenue, Brooklyn, was pulled from the Gowanus Canal at the foot of Bond Street, Brooklyn, a few minutes before 5 o'clock yesterday afternoon'."

So they hadn't been talking about me on my deck. Any fears about becoming dead fish food for dead fish in the Gowanus Canal that I might have developed on our funeral holiday were as nothing. The wise guys had been talking about the Jadrool, with him right there, making him sweat. They were waiting for him to do something stupid, but there he was, so they were speaking in code. Sort of. I offered the suggestion that Big Rosie had become a benefactor of a lot of Mafia orphans over the years; he did have a big heart, at least once the gunfire stopped.

"Probably," Chloe agreed.

Comforting. But it no longer mattered. We were all safe, if I was a little banged up. I had rediscovered my love for my wife, and had developed a good working friendship with The Cobra. Miracle was over her Italian phase, she said for good. "I think I'll try Chinese," she decided.

Bulpitt. He was just the same idiotic boorish man he had always been. Frankly, though, I thought I could see some humanizing taking place. Maybe the late Gertrude Hermione Dorcas Bulpitt had been the scourge of his life.

I did have one problem, though. I hadn't broken my ankle in crashing the L car so Captain Africa could be apprehended for an eventual gig in Her Majesty's prison system: I had only knocked myself out for a while. When I came to, I had also awakened to the fact that my talents were being wasted sitting in cars eight to twelve hours a day preparing UK residents to be at least a little less than deadly on UK roads. I had more to offer. Hadn't I solved this case with Chloe?

Well, no, I hadn't. Nor had she, although the cops gave her high marks for her contribution.

I was good at crashing cars, though, and not hurting anyone too much. But the UK didn't have a Hollywood, so there was little call for stunt drivers.

I could go back to the University of All That Glitters in the Collection Plate, but I didn't think they'd have me. Forget yoga. I never liked it. Dog-walking? Did I mention my wife's spending habits, and do you think that would suffice? Or being a sandwichboardman again? Please. What to do, what to do?

I was fretting over this after I got out of hospital as my wife and I went spending happily through the most recent and decidedly final guilt payment from Big Rosie. The hospital hadn't kept me long, just overnight because they said I had a slight concussion. I'd have gotten more rest at home; no Myron to pester me to tell him about drivers who were worse than he was. I only had one to tell him about, and it was via a phone call from a police driving examiner in London I had gotten while resting.

"A young woman was doing a police driving course," I began.

"I'd love to do one of those some day," Myron interjected. I silently screamed. They are the toughest of the tough.

"Anyway, she was approaching a cyclist who was very old and only doddering along at about 1 mile per hour. She was also driving on a road with a solid white line nearest to her. The examiner told her that if she crossed the solid line, he would fail her. So she drove for the next three miles at one mile per hour with a long queue of traffic building up behind her.

"She passed."

Myron had been impressed. It takes nerves of steel to hold up long lines of cars when it is nominally legal, when a road user is doing less than 10 miles per hour, to overtake them even if one must cross a double line to do it. Regarding double white lines, The Official Highway Code, Revised 2007 Edition, notes:

###

"You may cross the line if necessary provided the road is clear, to pass a stationary vehicle, or overtake a pedal cycle, horse or road maintenance vehicle, if they are travelling at 10 mph (16 km/h) or less." (Rule 139)

###

Why did the examiner tell her he'd fail her if she did something that is sanctioned by the official rule book? Darned if I know.

In a way, it was too bad my profession annoyed me while I was supposed to be resting. Without the guilt money from Big Rosie, one of us had to earn a living, and it looked as if it would be me. Again. Sure, I could hire Biff out as a guard dog, but he will ignore anything for food. Mr. Bumpy was useless, which is what cats are made for. He was handsome, though. Maybe I could get him gigs in TV adverts. Doubtful.

My wife wasn't much of a cook, except for those few Italian dishes, so hiring her out as a personal chef didn't seem to fit the bill. She had a university degree, but it was a couple of decades old, and she had never really put it to use because of Big Rosie's generosity. Sure, she had seen all the capitals of Europe and their great artworks before we met, had volunteered at organizations helping everything from donkeys to zebras, but had no *bona fide* work experience.

I was pondering my options, including returning to the Pits of Bul, when Chloe solved my problems during one of her increasingly frequent visits.

"I wonder if you would consider working with me?" she asked about ten days later, as I was obsessively number-crunching and my wife was cooking up some luganica left from the batch she had frozen when the late Alphonse Eugene Melanzane—Big Rosie—had smuggled it in from the States. I didn't ask how, but who would have noticed a money belt or two stuffed with it, on his humongous body (god rest his soul) and what with his habitual garlic breath?

"I'll think about it," I said. "I'm afraid my resume is getting too long, and people will think I'm a dilettante."

My wife snorted, and kept on stirring. "Chloe," she called out. "Can you stay to dinner?"

What was this? They REALLY were lifelong friends?

Screwed. But yes. The answer to The Cobra's question, I decided, was yes.

FINITO!

Rat Bastards

What is Shelf Barker going to do now? Does he give up his career as a driving instructor, in test-happy Britain a sinecure for life? Does he investigate heinous crimes along with ex-wife The Cobra?

Turn the page for a hint….

Rat Bastards

By Nicky McBride

CHAPTER ONE

One-Trick Pony

I jumped about ten feet in the air. No, that's wrong. I was stuck under the steering wheel of my trusty L car, dozing, across the street from a terraced house I was watching during the noonday shift. I was looking for signs that one of its occupants was cavorting with a lady not his wife.

What I meant to say was that I would have jumped ten feet in the air if I could have. As it was, my herky-jerky motion (with apologies to Paul Simon for borrowing his phrase), simply knocked my coffee off the dashboard onto my semi-clean khakis and, as well, onto some important papers. Well, important to the future drivers of the United Kingdom of Great Britain, Northern Ireland, Scotland, Wales and sometimes—or so the dingbat separatists claim with all the power of a mosquito in November—the Ancient Kingdom of Cornwall. The papers were the most recent Fail sheets of prospective drivers who had not managed to charm the examiner sufficiently to pass and add their lunacy to our roadways, or whose driving skills—after 20 hours tuition with yours truly—had not risen to the level demanded by the world's most difficult driving test. Truly. Only South Africa's driving test might be worse. Most people there simply avoid the issue and drive without official government sanction. I've been told. In the UK? Not so much, I've been told. The penalties are too stiff.

Since I was still working eight-hour days for Cars from 'L —and moonlighting morning, noon and night as the trusty Number Two in BarkerBarker Investigations Ltd.—I had dozed off. I was, therefore, surprised when Number One of BarkerBarker tapped me on the shoulder. Chloe Barker, ex-wife number three, had the look of love in her eyes. Not for me. Not at all, not for years. That look could mean only one thing: a juicy case, something to sink our teeth into after several months of lurking behind garbage trucks, wielding our mobile phones for on-the-hoof photos of gypsies, tramps and thieves who were wanted by spouses, parents, pissed off business partners or the police.

"Shelf, it figures," she snarled, hands on hips, cigarette hanging from her luridly lipsticked cartilage-enhanced full lower lip, and that squinty-eyed assessment look I knew so well.

I lied about everything except the look. Chloe didn't smoke and she couldn't very well strike that pose with her almost six-foot height scrunched down to look me in the eyes in the de rigueur Ford Fiesta learner car. Her lips were all natural, and no more nor less appealing than the next woman's.

This could only mean one thing. We had a live one. Or perhaps, better, a dead one. As it turned out, just like our very first case together if you wish to dignify it thus, we had *two* dead ones.

Best of all, as it happens, they were in the Ancient Kingdom of Cornwall. Call it a mini-holiday. Call it what you will. I would have leapt in the air and clicked my heels for joy if I could, even if I hadn't been cramped into the cheapmobile. I'm sort of spastic, if truth be known, and conducting yoga classes back when I plied that trade was about as much physical prowess as my tall, spindly, wasted-looking phys could muster. Without doubt, a chance to investigate the deaths of two unfortunates by the seaside was reason for rejoicing. My wife and I had been on a short financial leash since her benevolent uncle, the Mafia don, had died so suddenly. Big Rosie, a/k/a Alphonse Eugene Melanzane, took his largesse to the grave along with his large-*ness*, all nicely packaged in a slightly dented mahogany eternity bed. OK, I'm not proud of my part in his casket rolling down the church steps and into the street, but what can you do? I am what I am and that's all what I am, as Popeye used to say. (Small favours. My wife does NOT look like Olive Oyl. Not at all.)

TO BE CONTINUED...